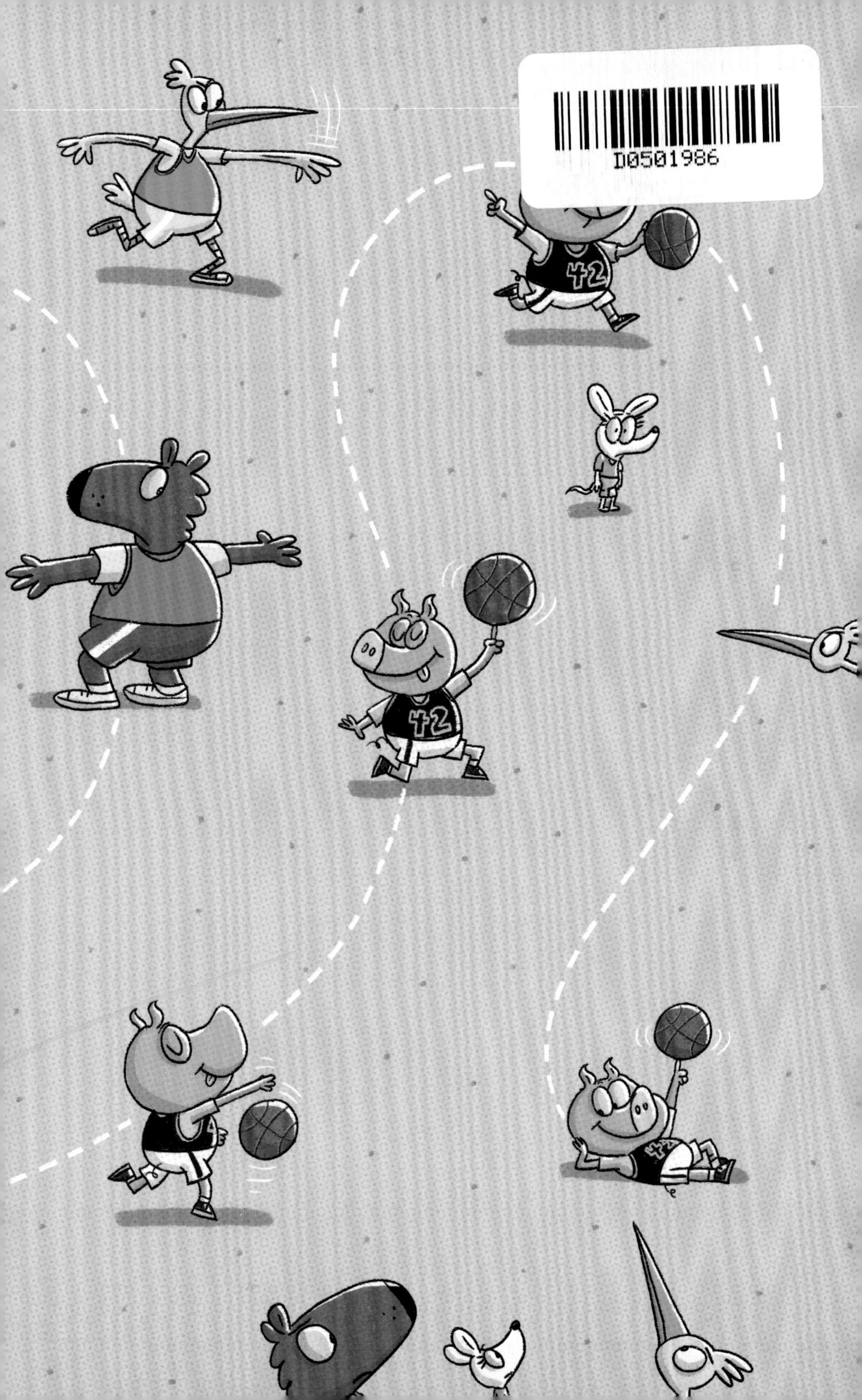
42
42
42

I Like to Read® Comics instill confidence and the joy of reading in new readers.
Created by award-winning artists as well as talented newcomers, these imaginative
books support beginners' reading comprehension with extensive visual support.

We hope that all new readers will say, "I like to read comics!"

Visit our website for flash cards, activities, and more about the I Like to Read® series:
www.holidayhouse.com/ILiketoRead
#ILTR

I LIKE TO READ is a registered trademark of Holiday House Publishing, Inc.

Copyright © 2022 by Ethan Long
All Rights Reserved
HOLIDAY HOUSE is registered in the U.S. Patent and Trademark Office.
Printed and bound in February 2022 at C&C Offset, Shenzhen, China.
The artwork was created digitally.
www.holidayhouse.com
First Edition
1 3 5 7 9 10 8 6 4 2

Library of Congress Cataloging-in-Publication Data is available.

ISBN: 978-0-8234-5148-7 (hardcover)

HOGGY WENT-A- COURTIN'

Ethan Long

I Like to Read COMICS™

HOLIDAY HOUSE · NEW YORK

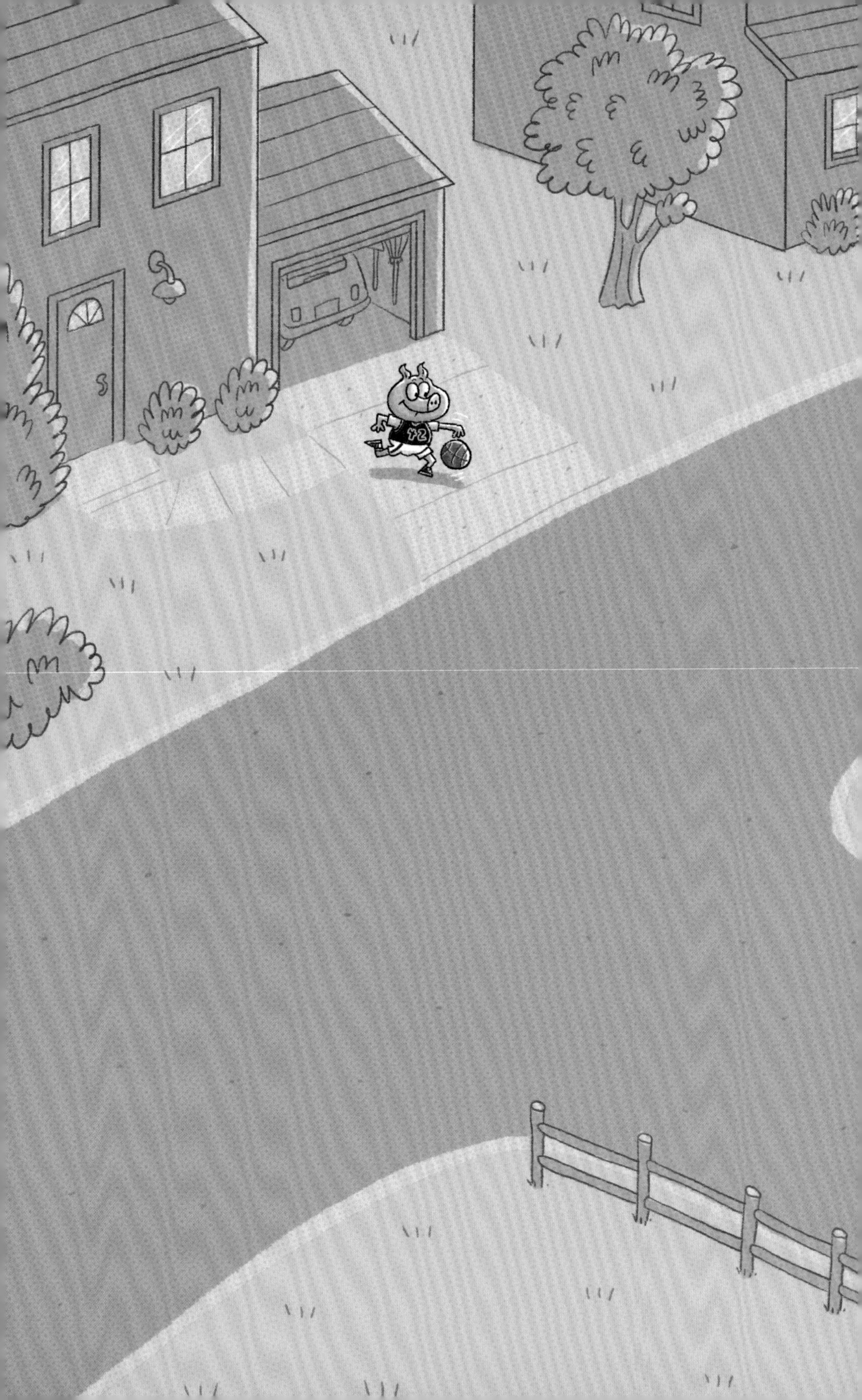

42

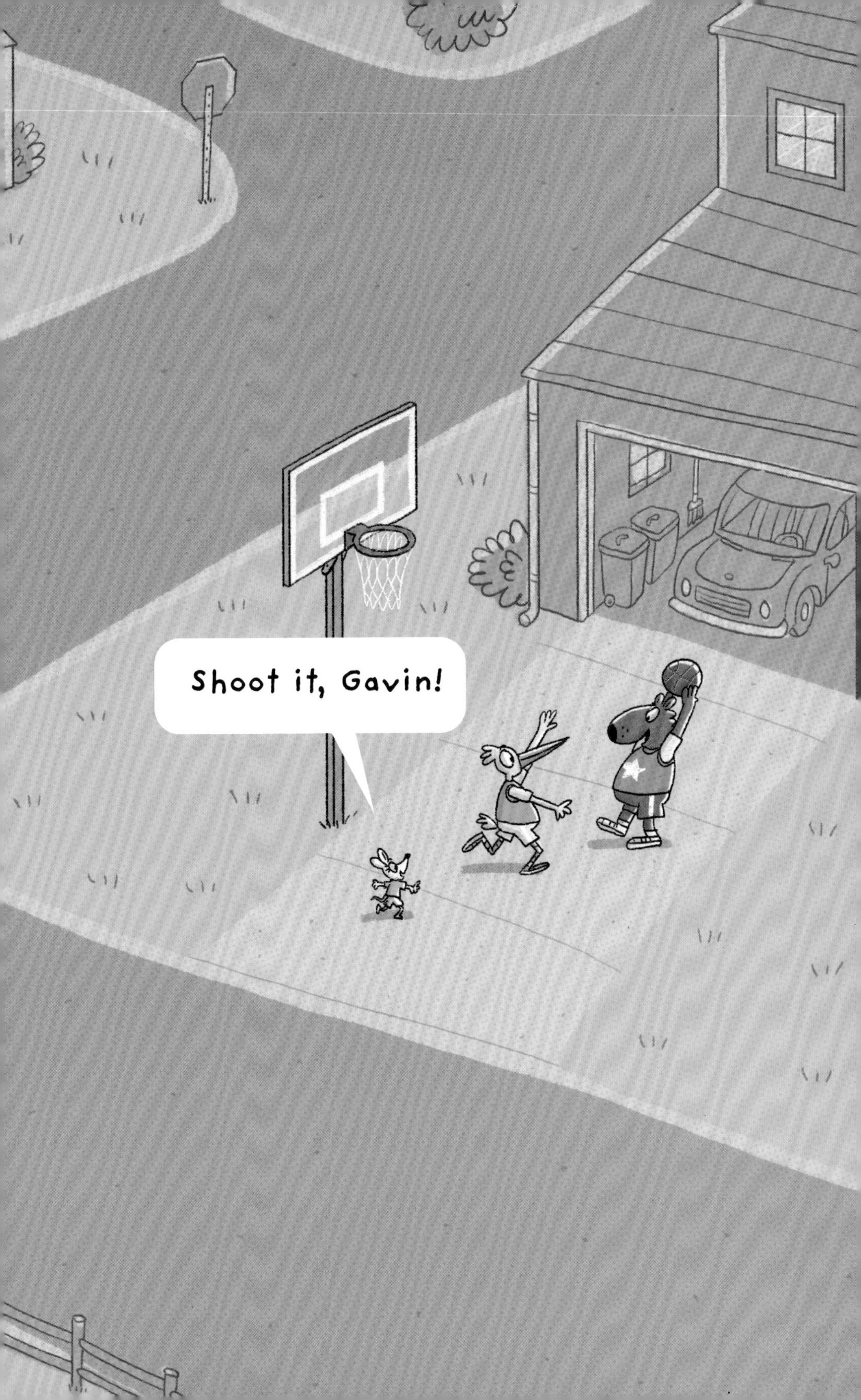
Shoot it, Gavin!

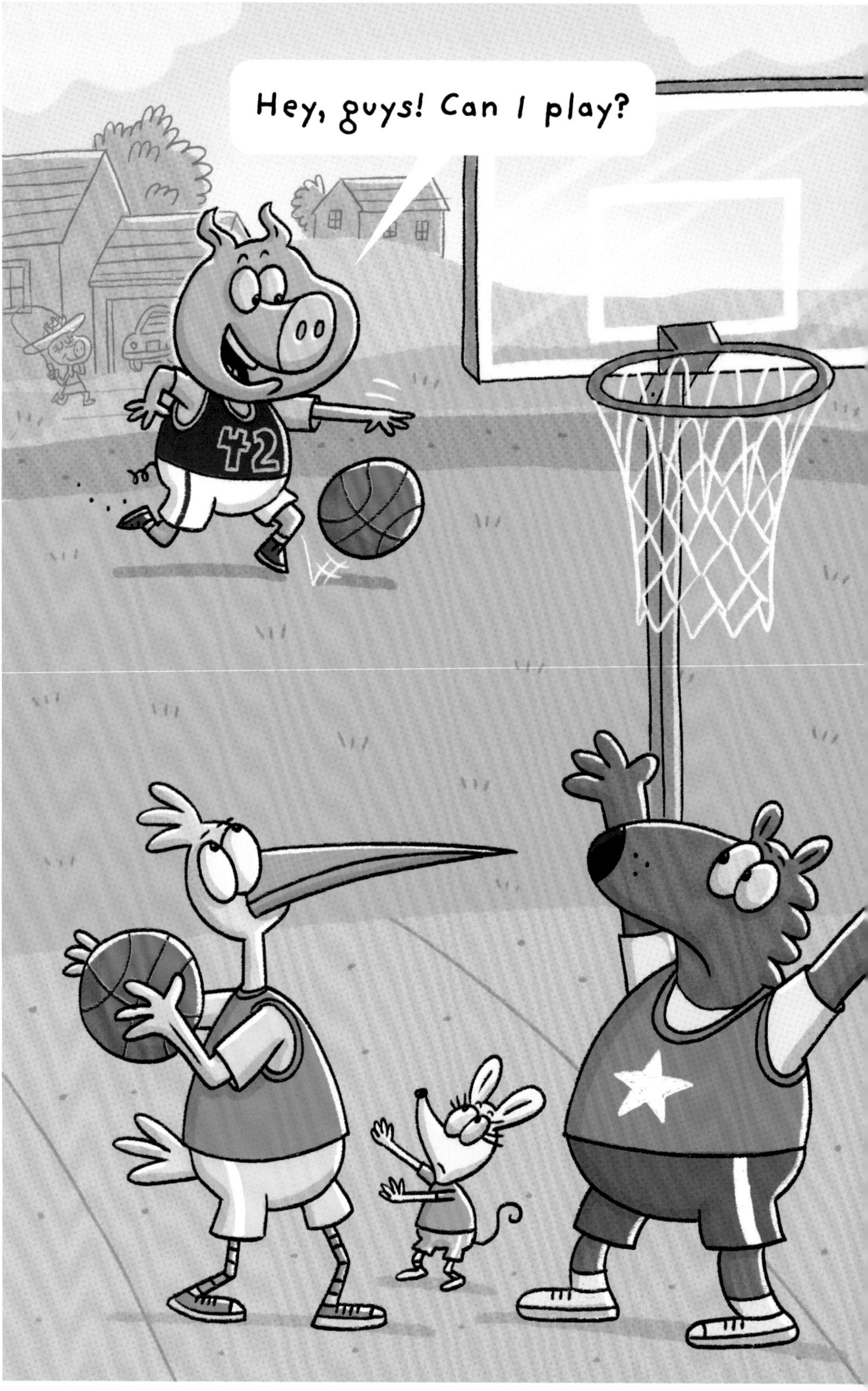
Hey, guys! Can I play?
42

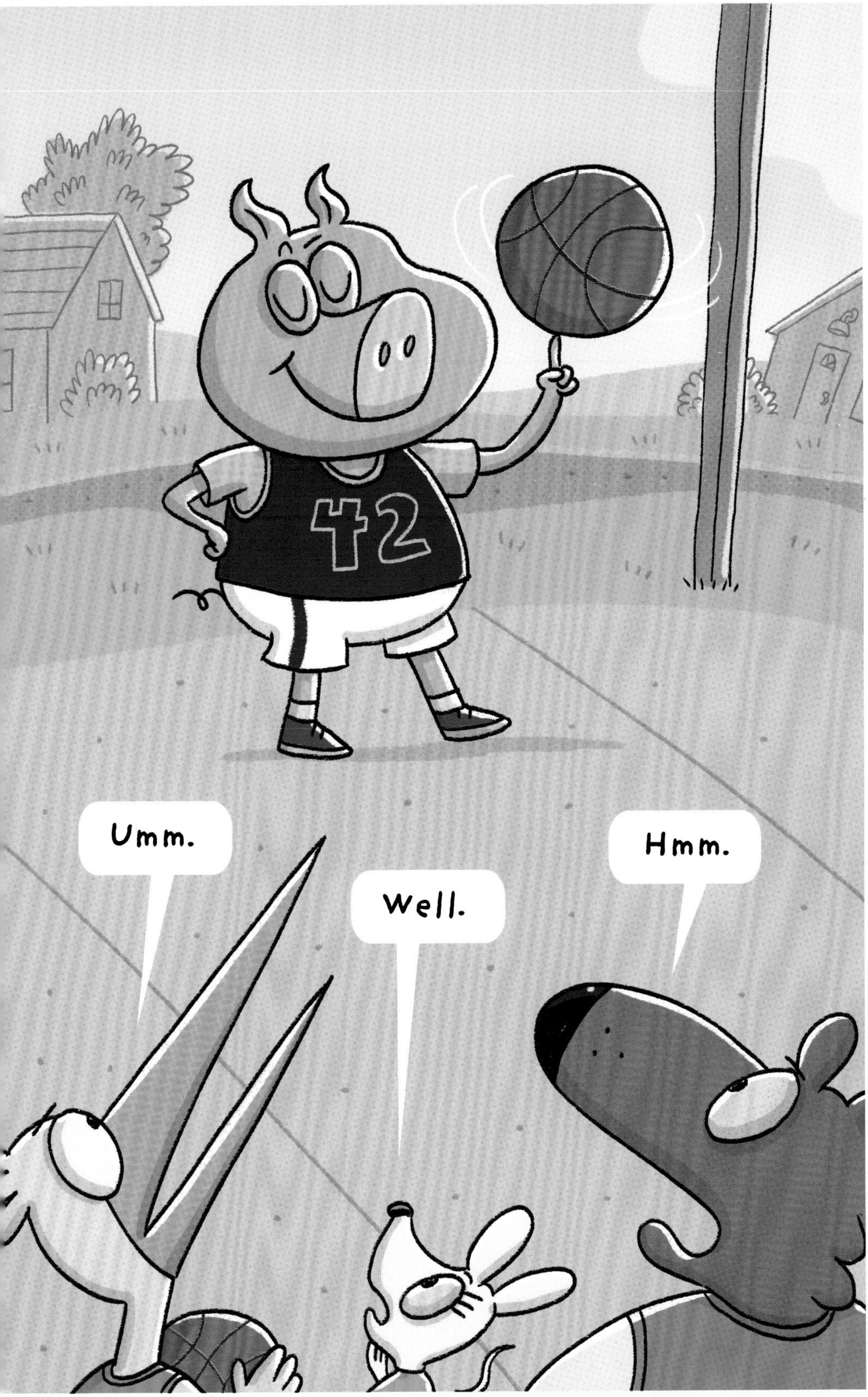
42
Umm.
Well.
Hmm.

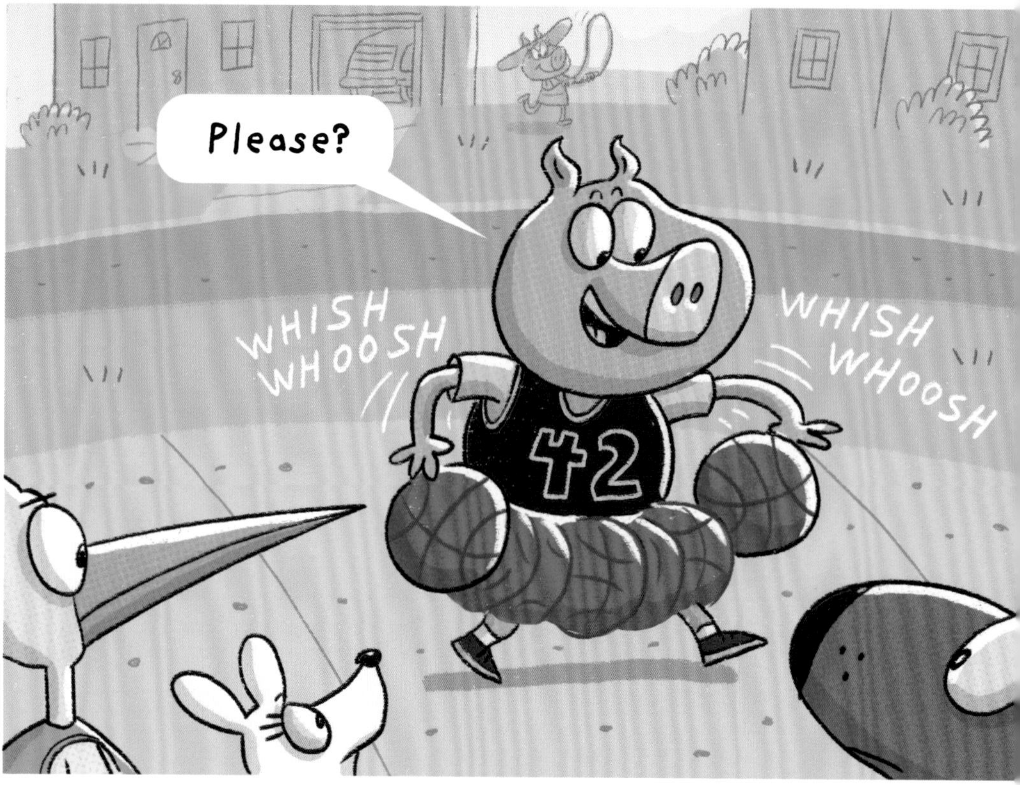
Please?
WHISH WHOOSH
WHISH WHOOSH

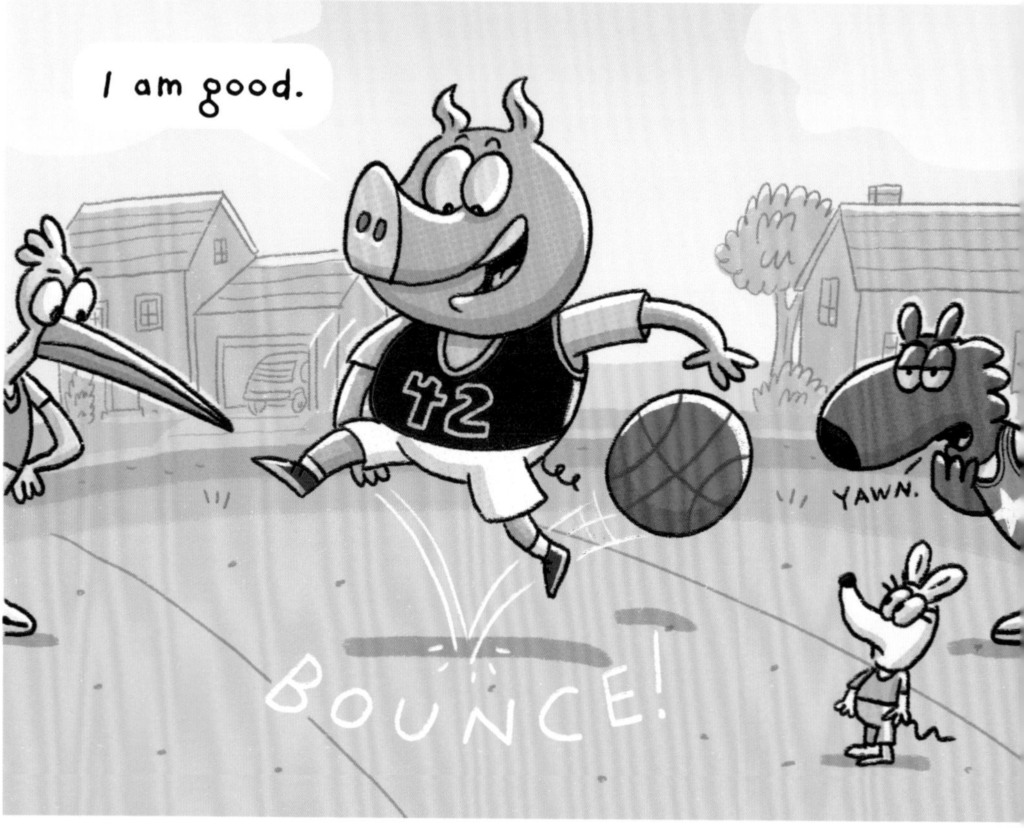
I am good.
YAWN.
BOUNCE!

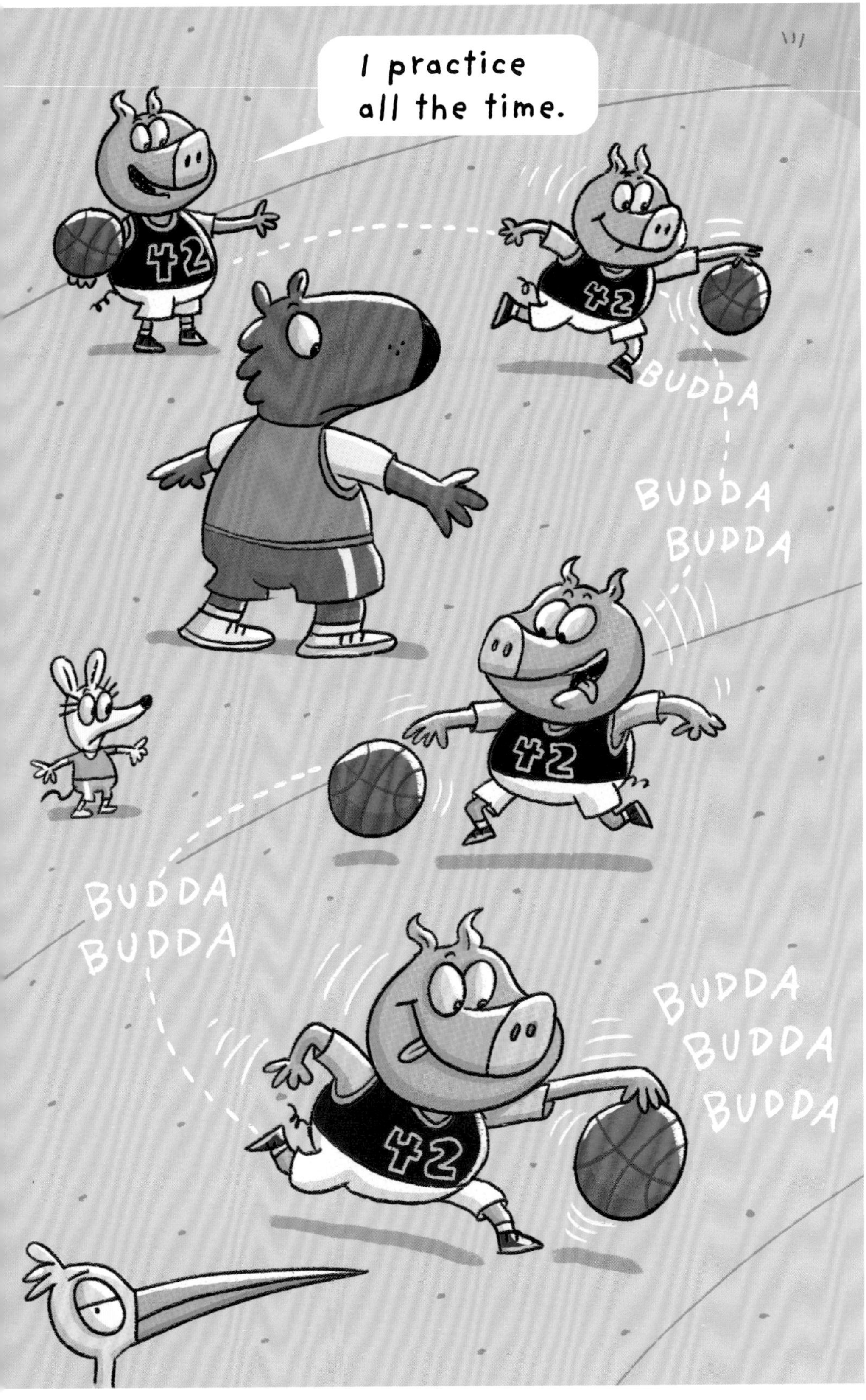
I practice
all the time.
BUDDA
BUDDA
BUDDA
BUDDA
BUDDA
BUDDA
BUDDA
BUDDA

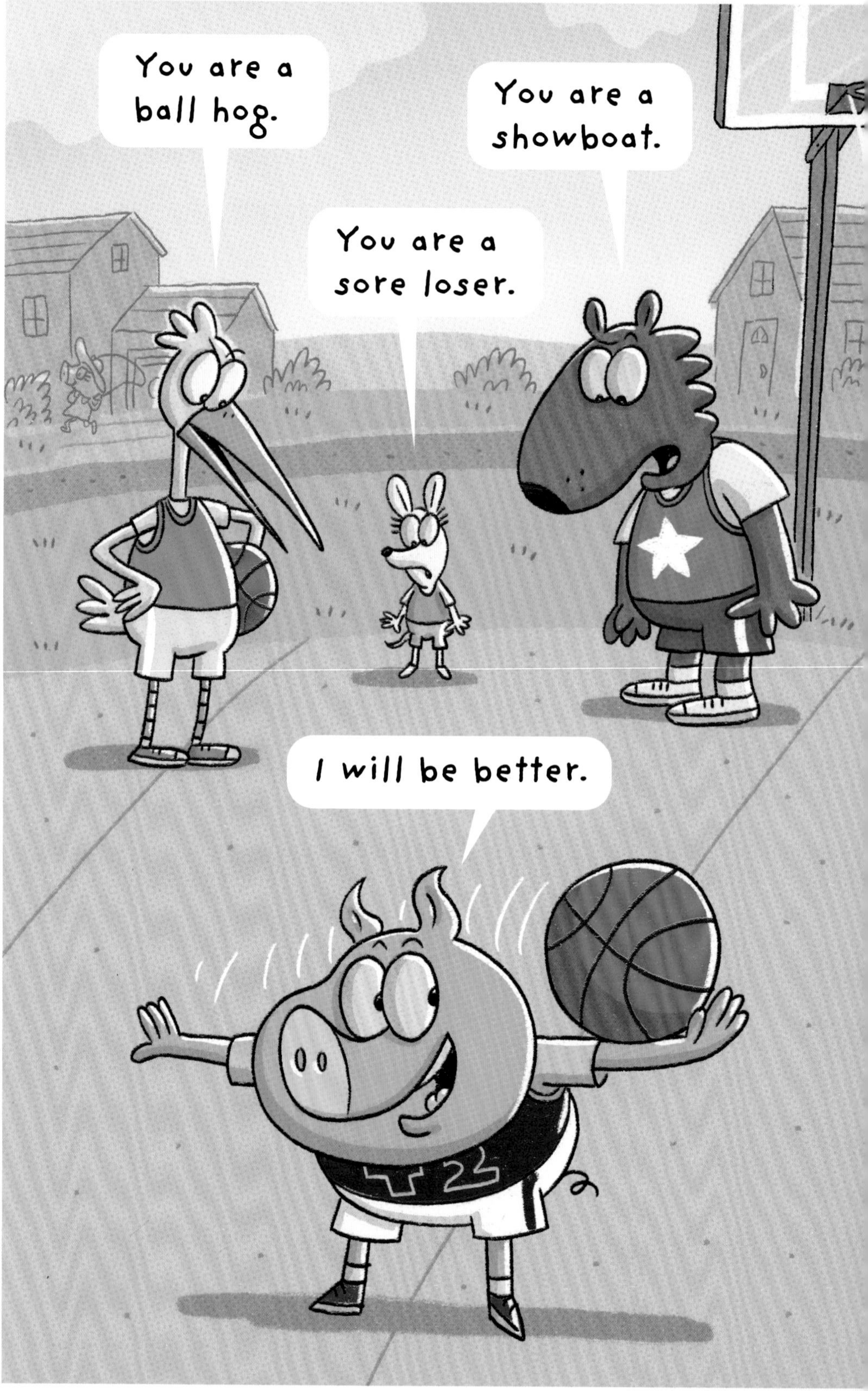
You are a ball hog.
You are a sore loser.
You are a showboat.
I will be better.

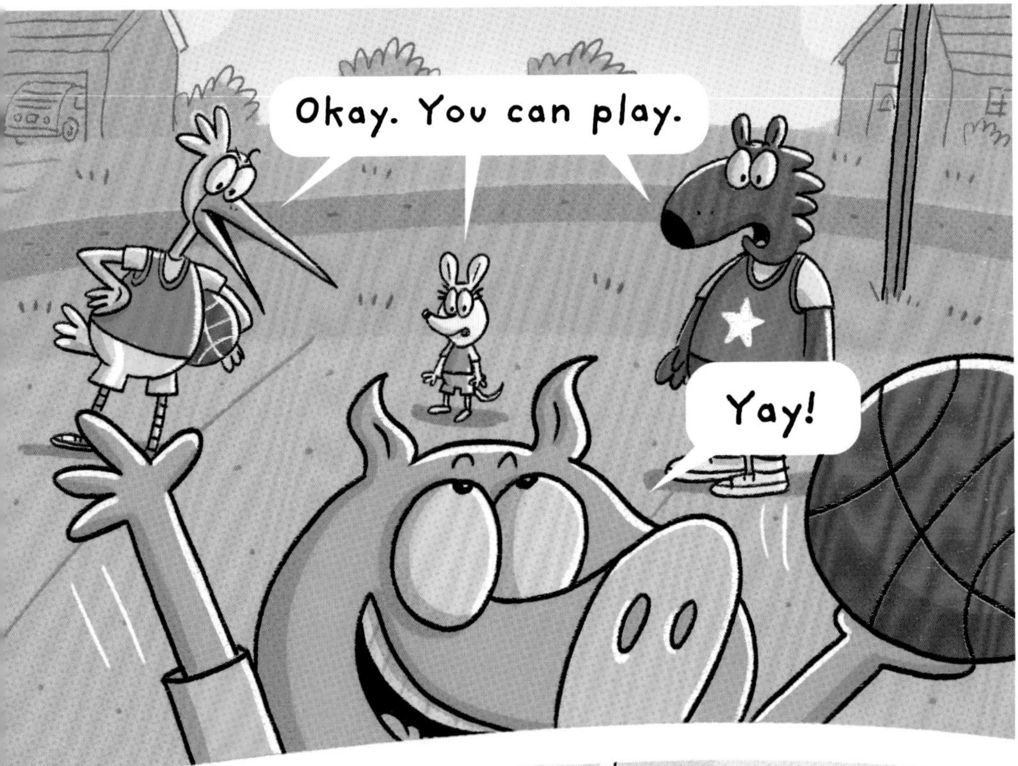
Okay. You can play.
Yay!

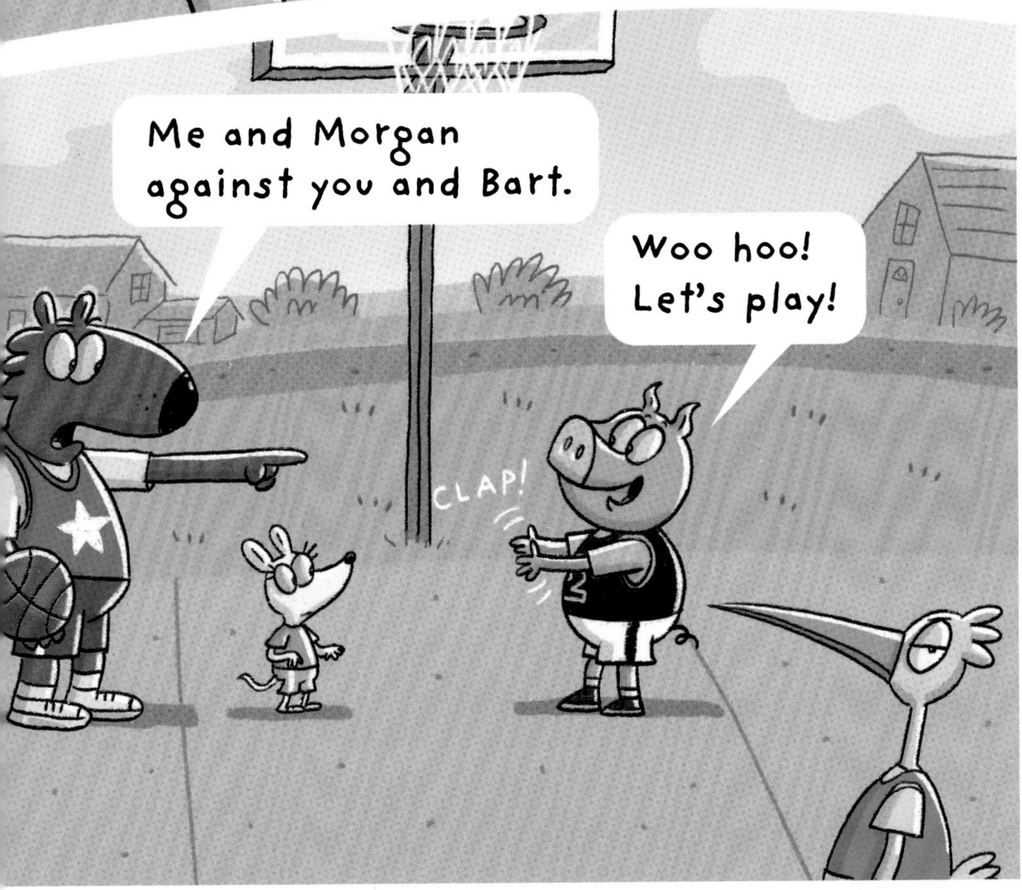
Me and Morgan against you and Bart.
Woo hoo! Let's play!
CLAP!

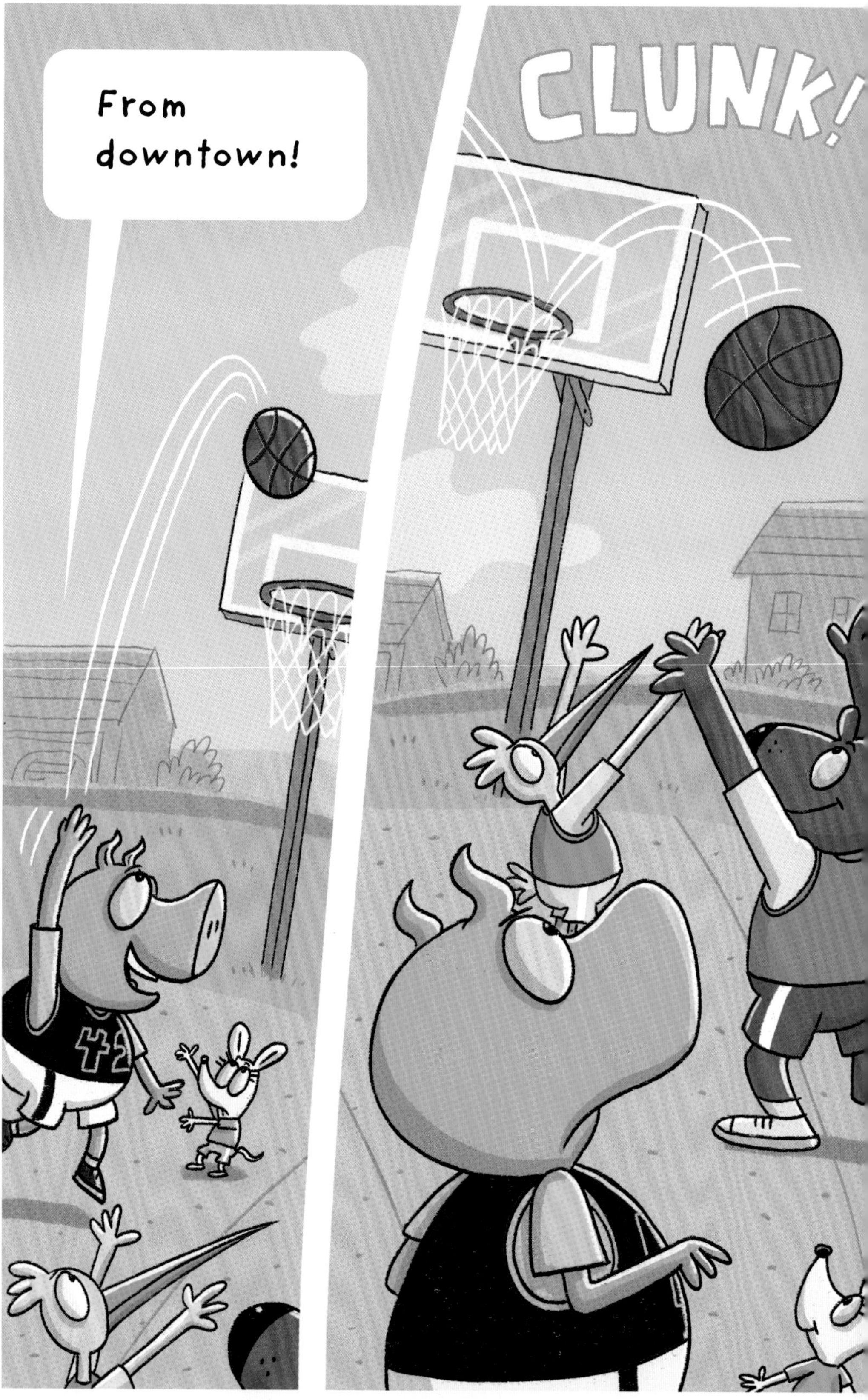
From downtown!
CLUNK!
42

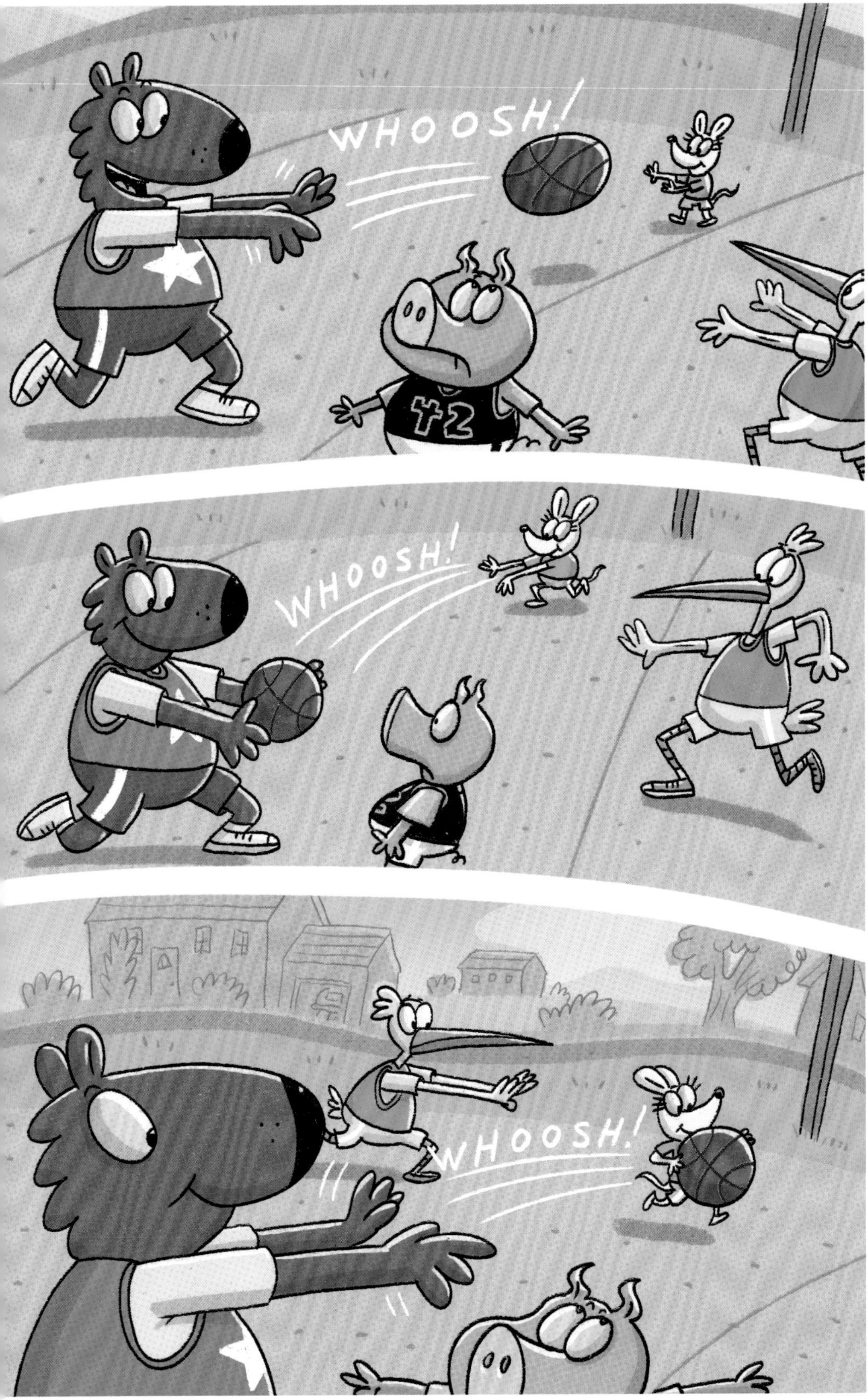
WHOOSH!
42
WHOOSH!
WHOOSH!

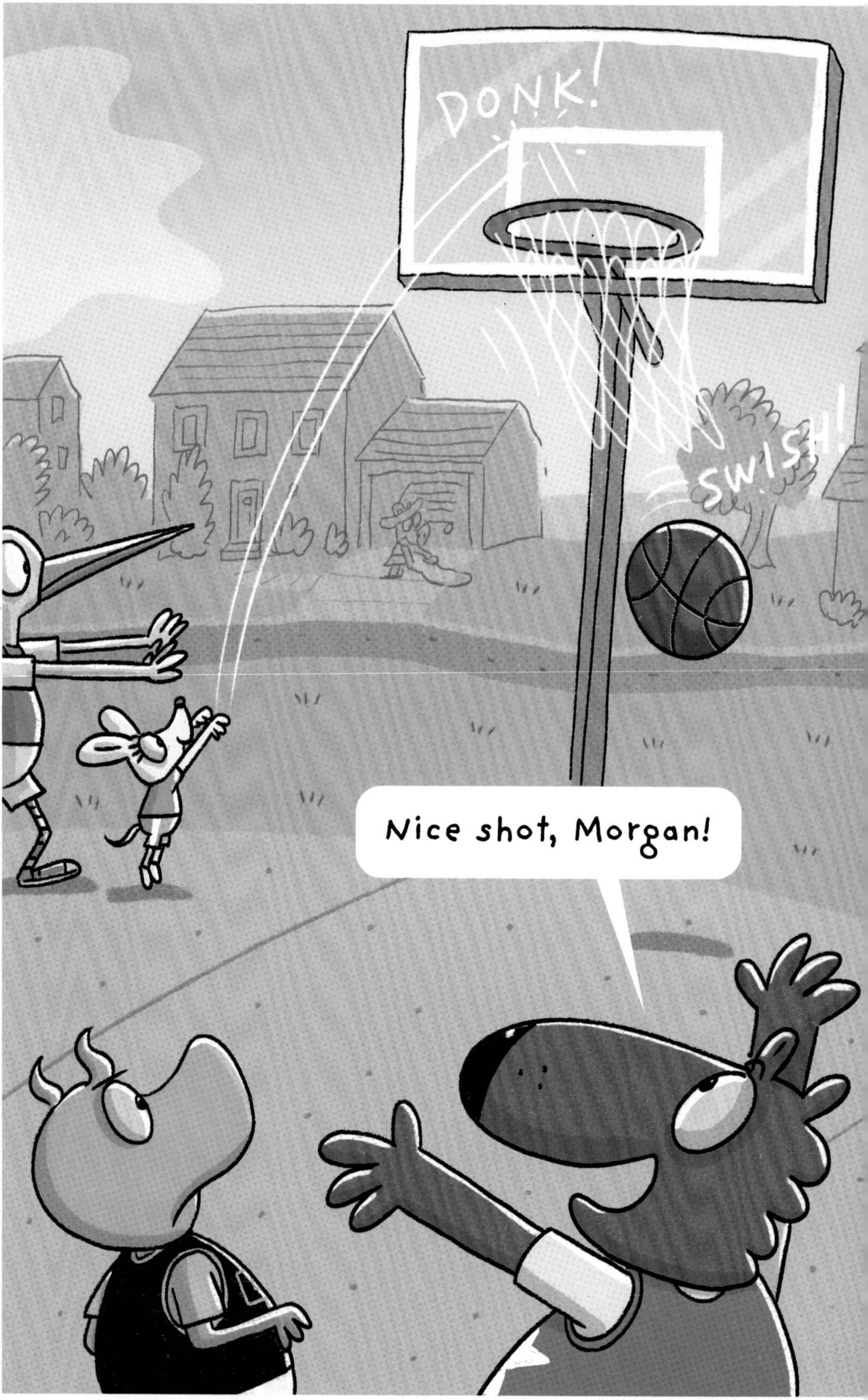
DONK!
SWISH!
Nice shot, Morgan!

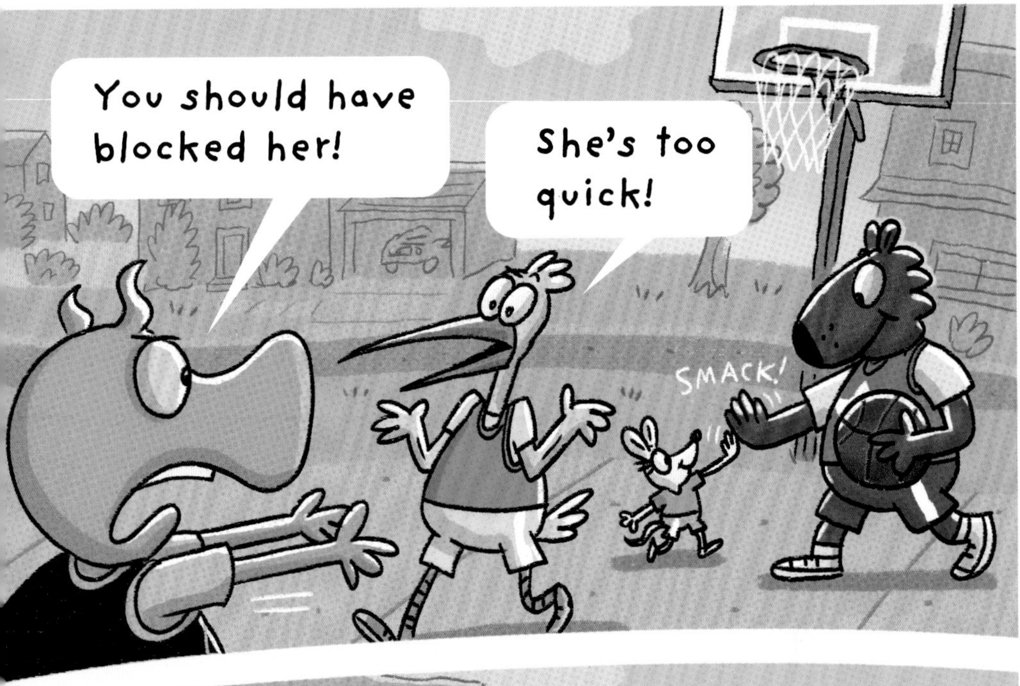
You should have blocked her!
She's too quick!
SMACK!

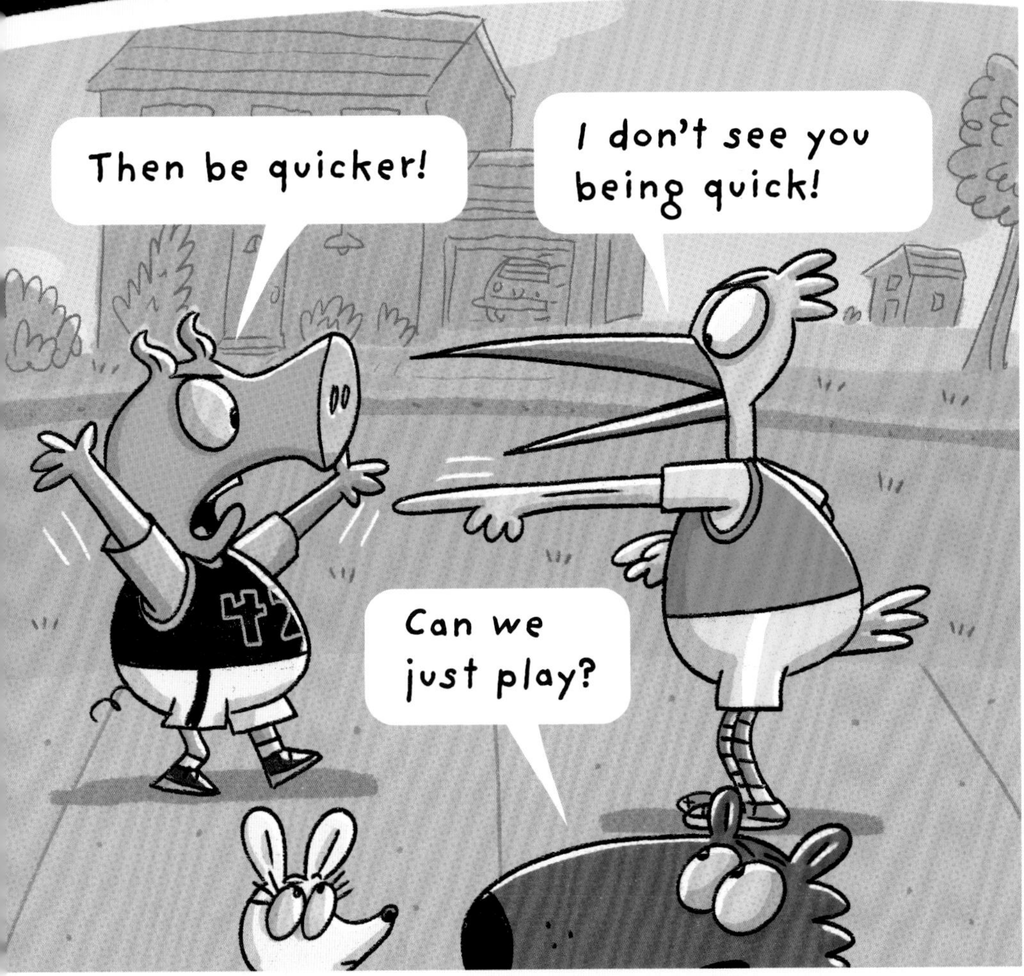
Then be quicker!
I don't see you being quick!
Can we just play?

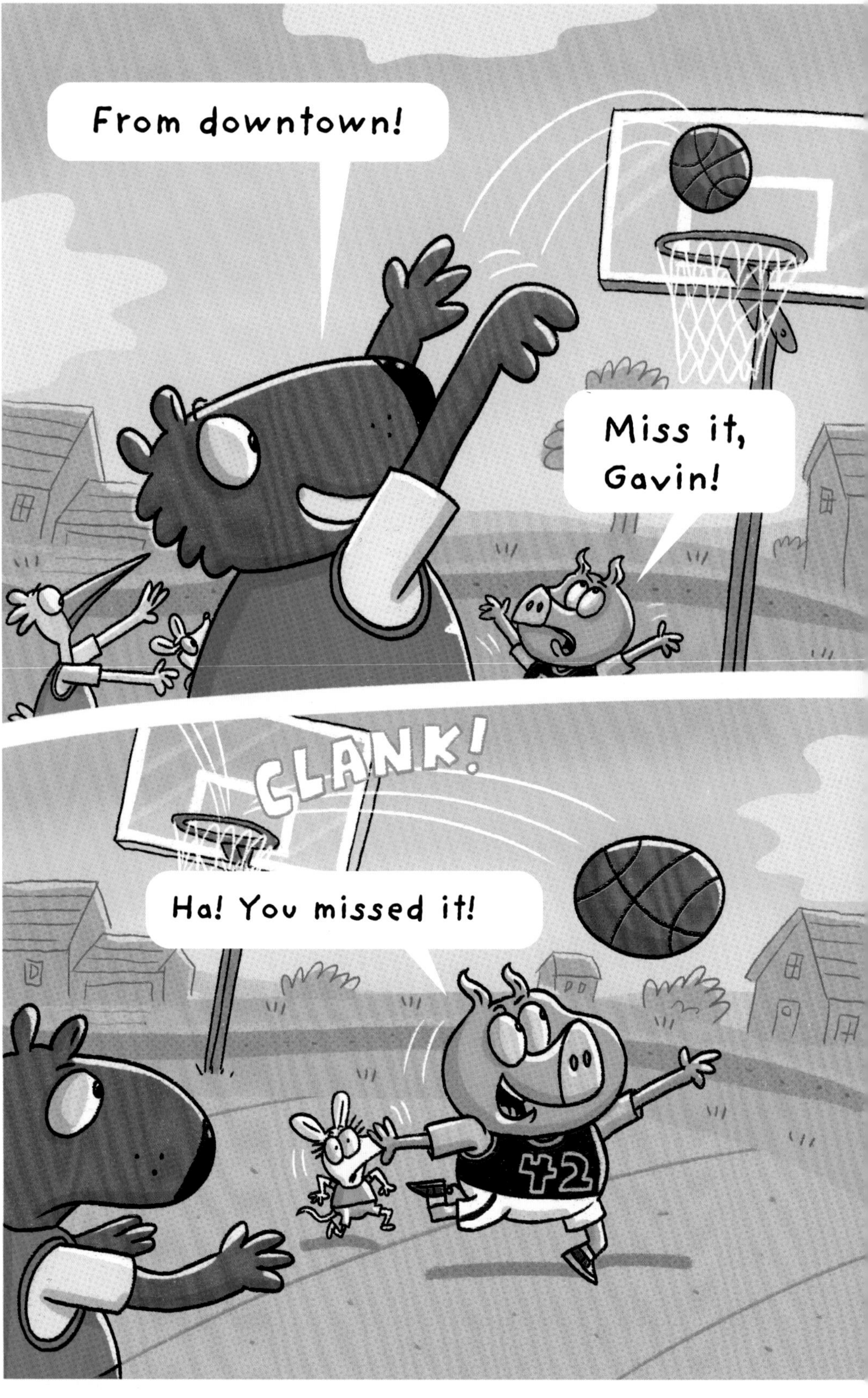
From downtown!
Miss it, Gavin!
CLANK!
Ha! You missed it!

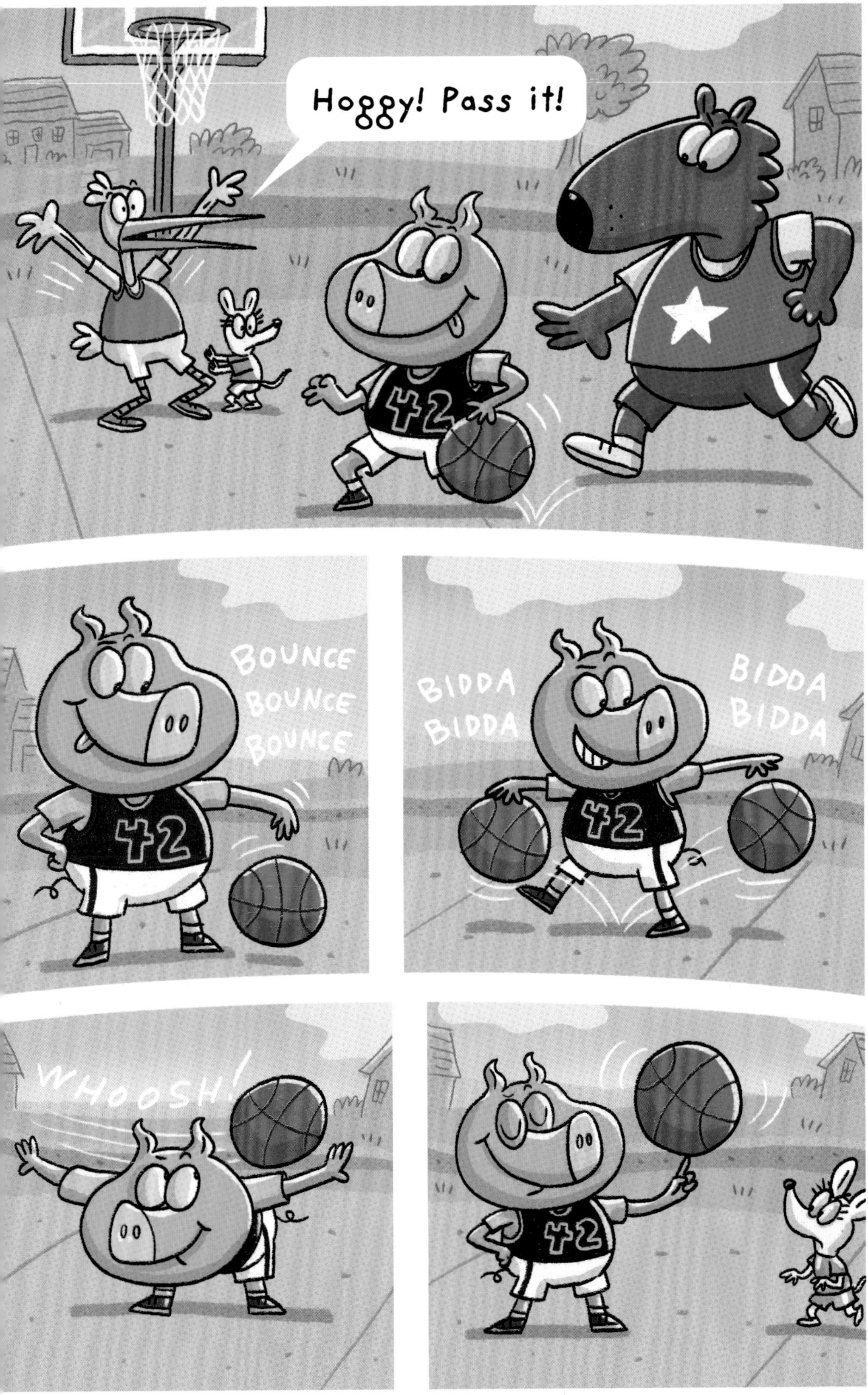
Hoggy! Pass it!
BOUNCE
BOUNCE
BOUNCE
BIDDA
BIDDA
BIDDA
BIDDA
WHOOSH!

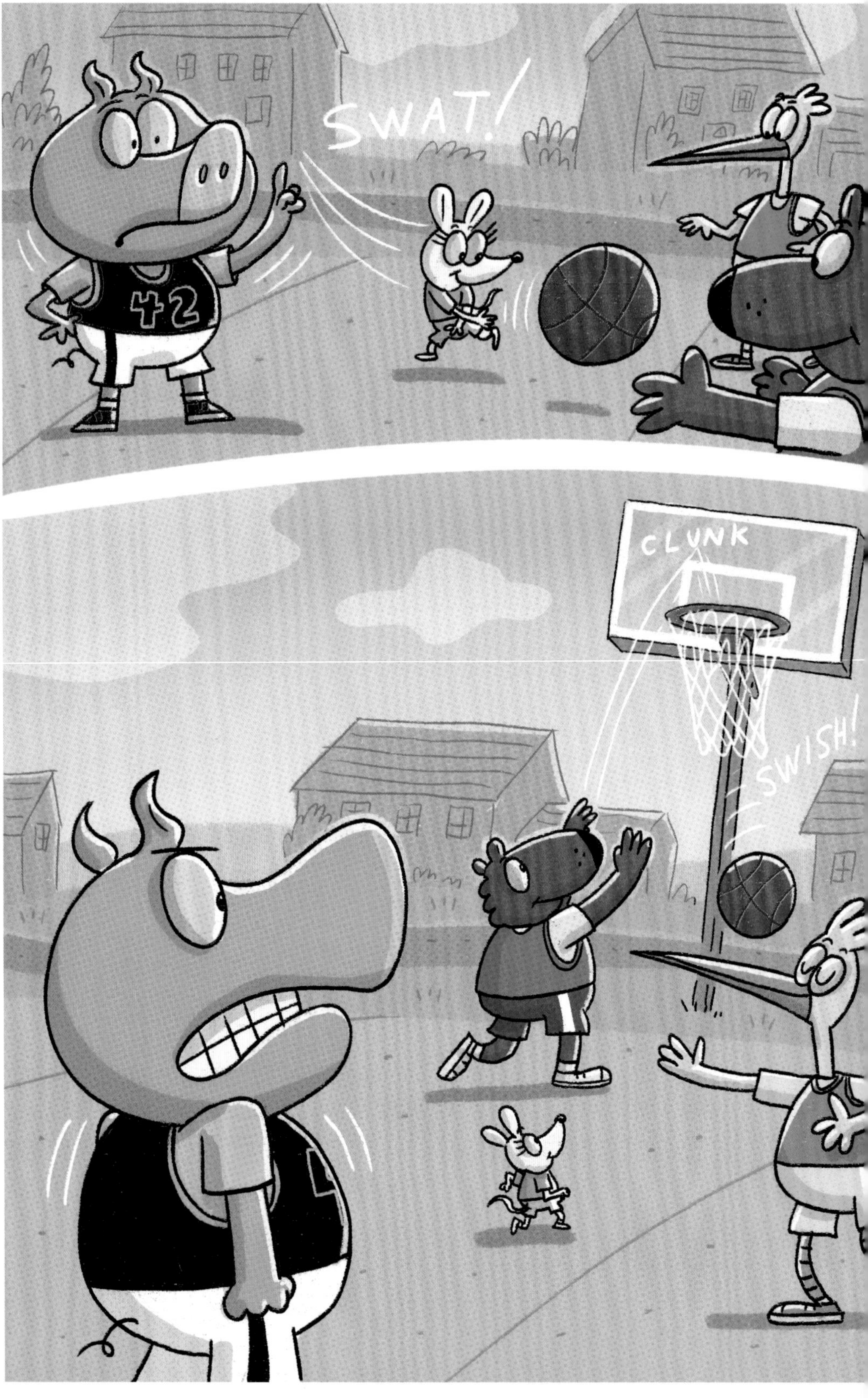
SWAT!
42
CLUNK
SWISH!

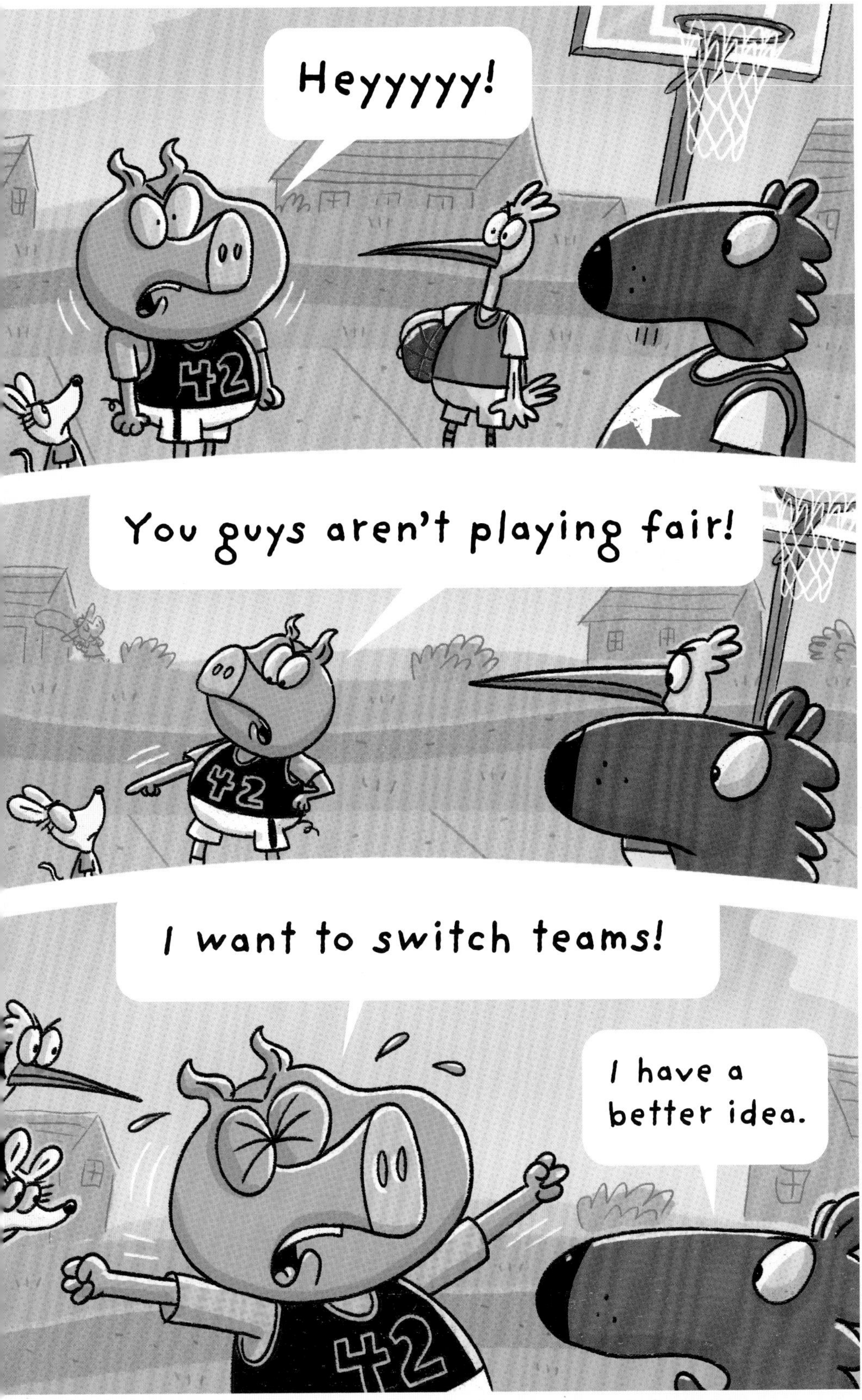

Heyyyyy!
You guys aren't playing fair!
I want to switch teams!
I have a better idea.

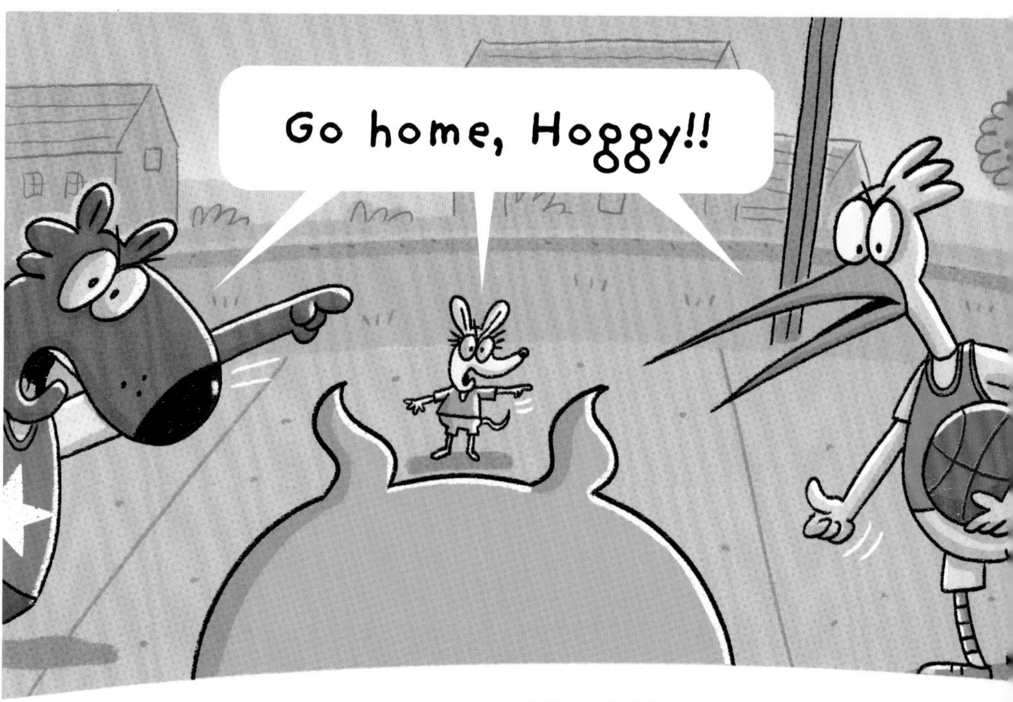
Go home, Hoggy!!

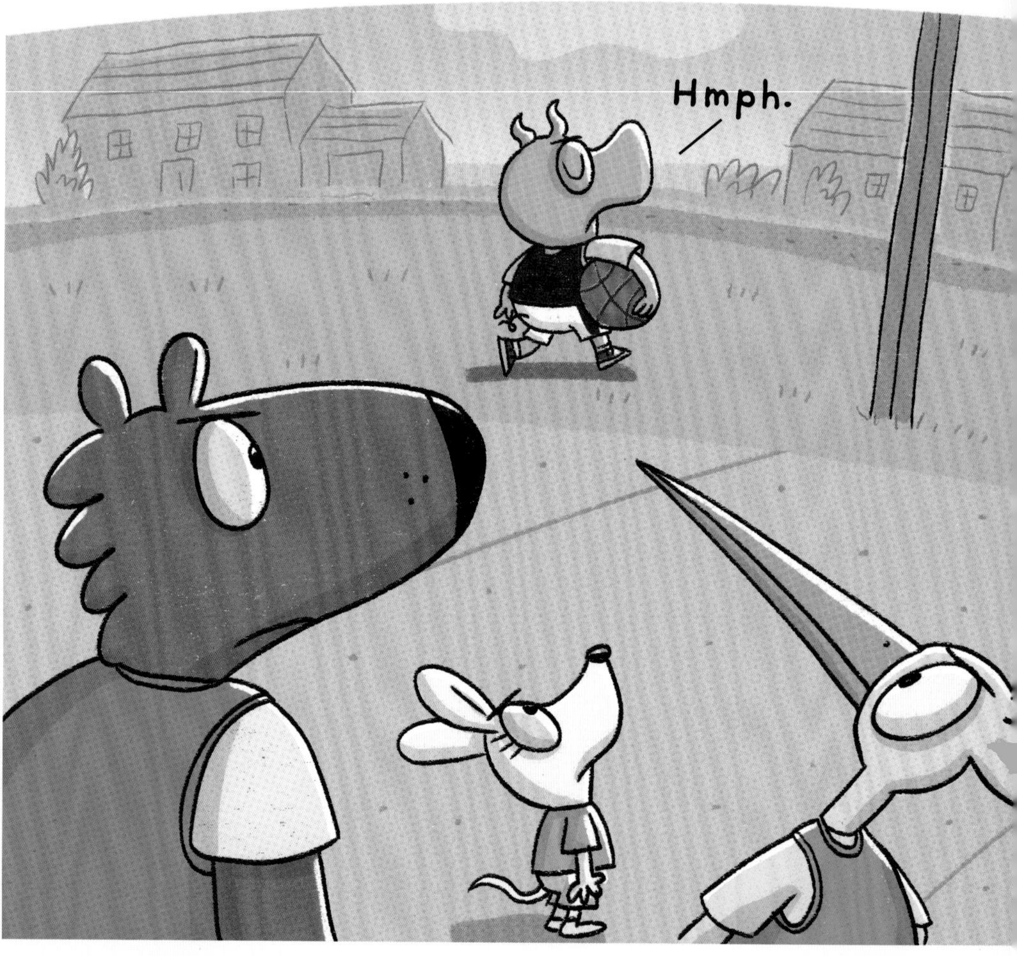
Hmph.

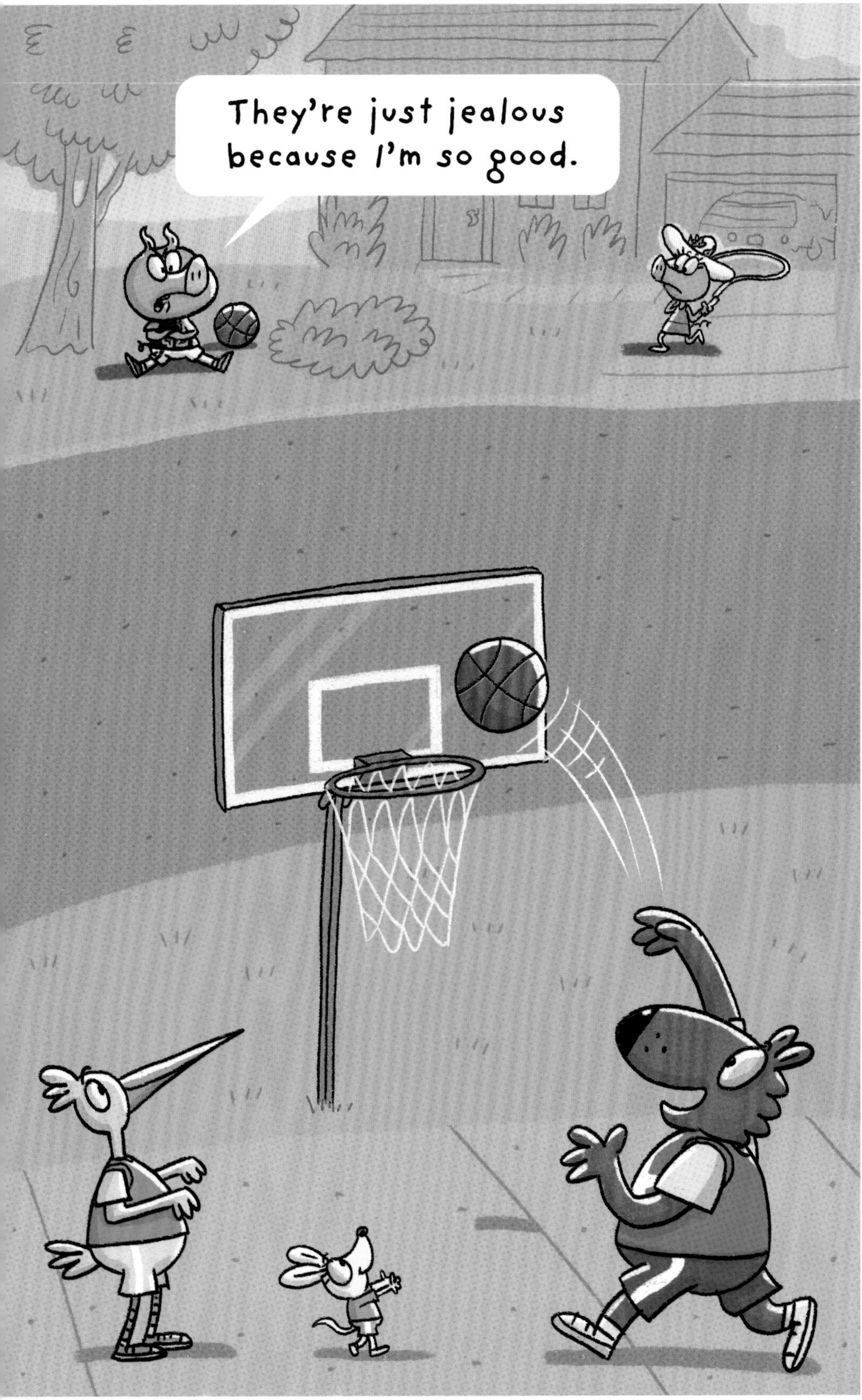
They're just jealous because I'm so good.

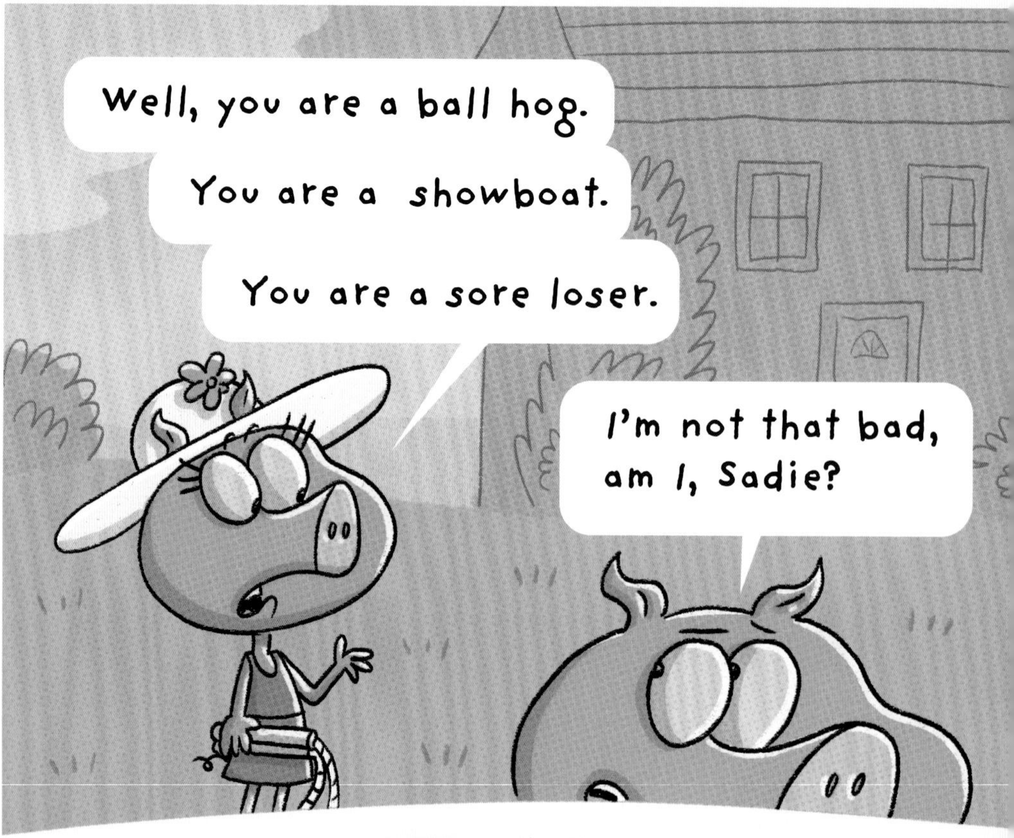
Well, you are a ball hog.
You are a showboat.
You are a sore loser.
I'm not that bad, am I, Sadie?

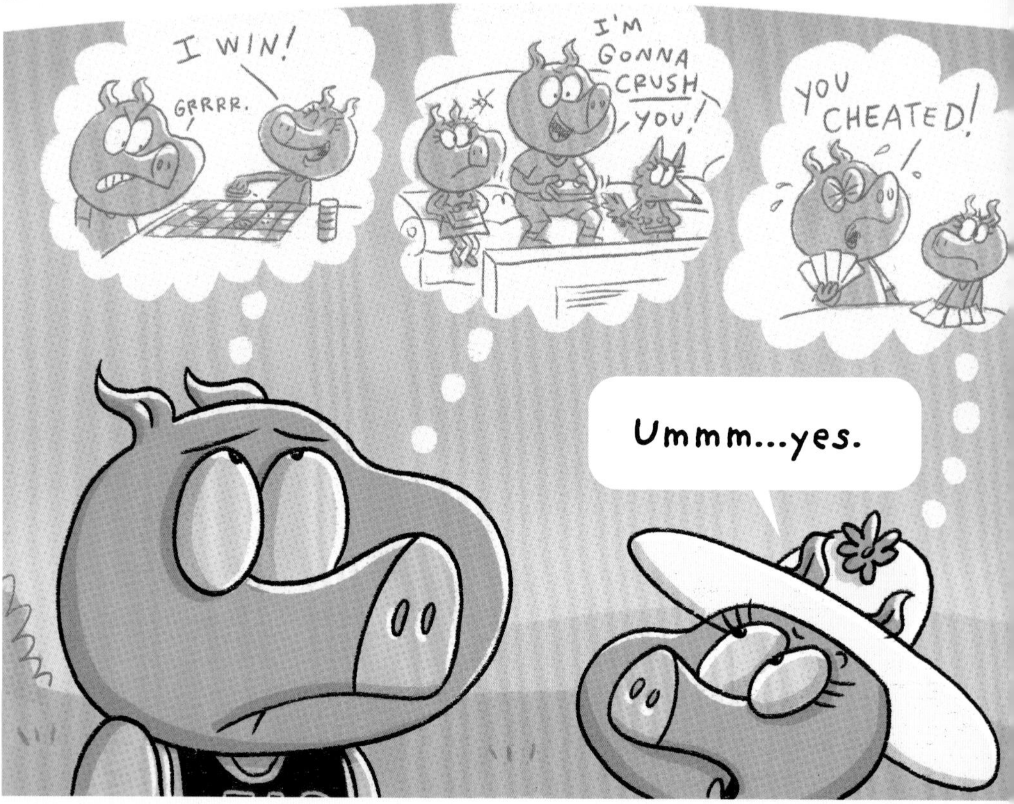
I WIN!
GRRRR.
I'M GONNA CRUSH YOU!
YOU CHEATED!
Ummm...yes.

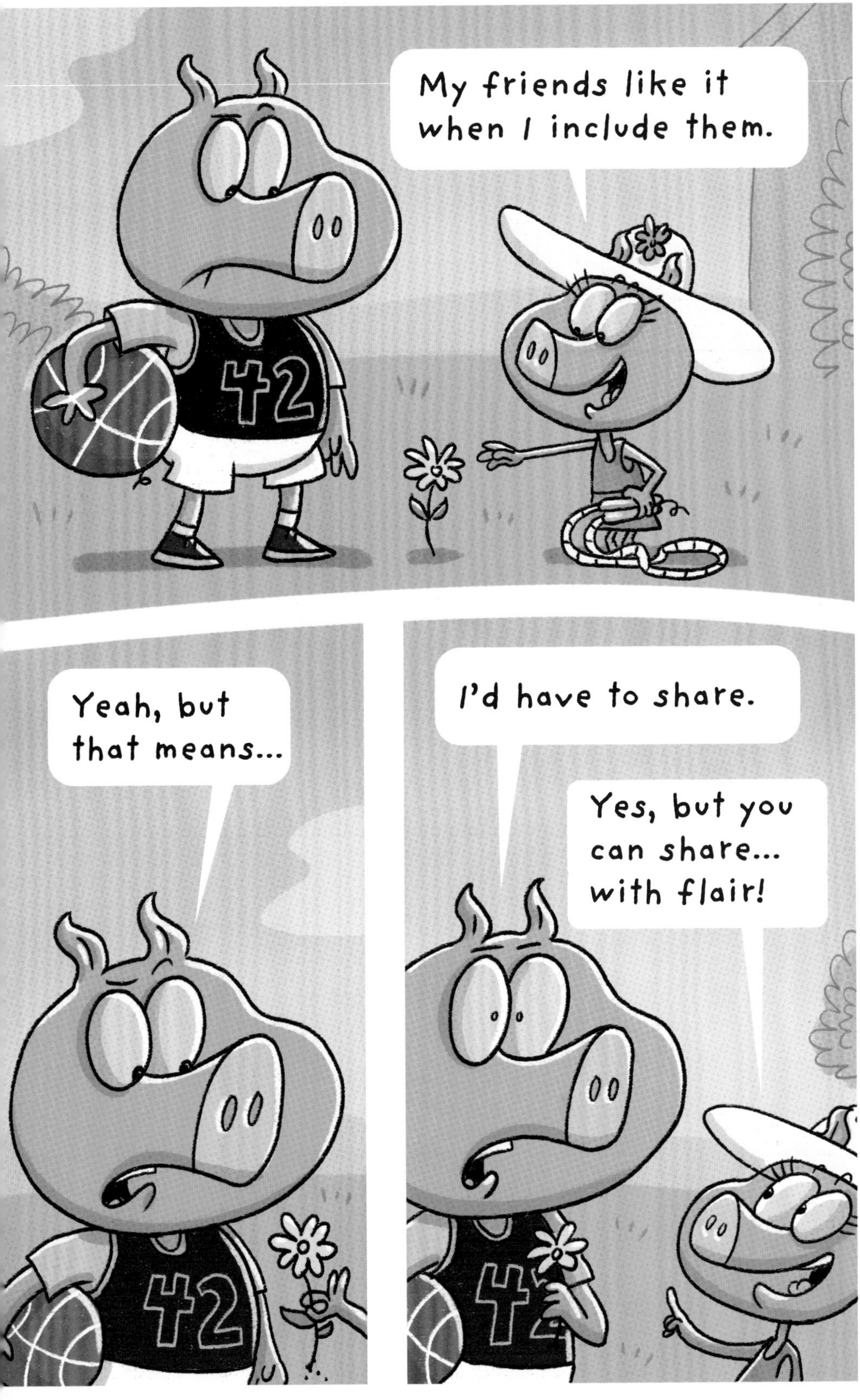
My friends like it when I include them.
Yeah, but that means...
I'd have to share.
Yes, but you can share... with flair!

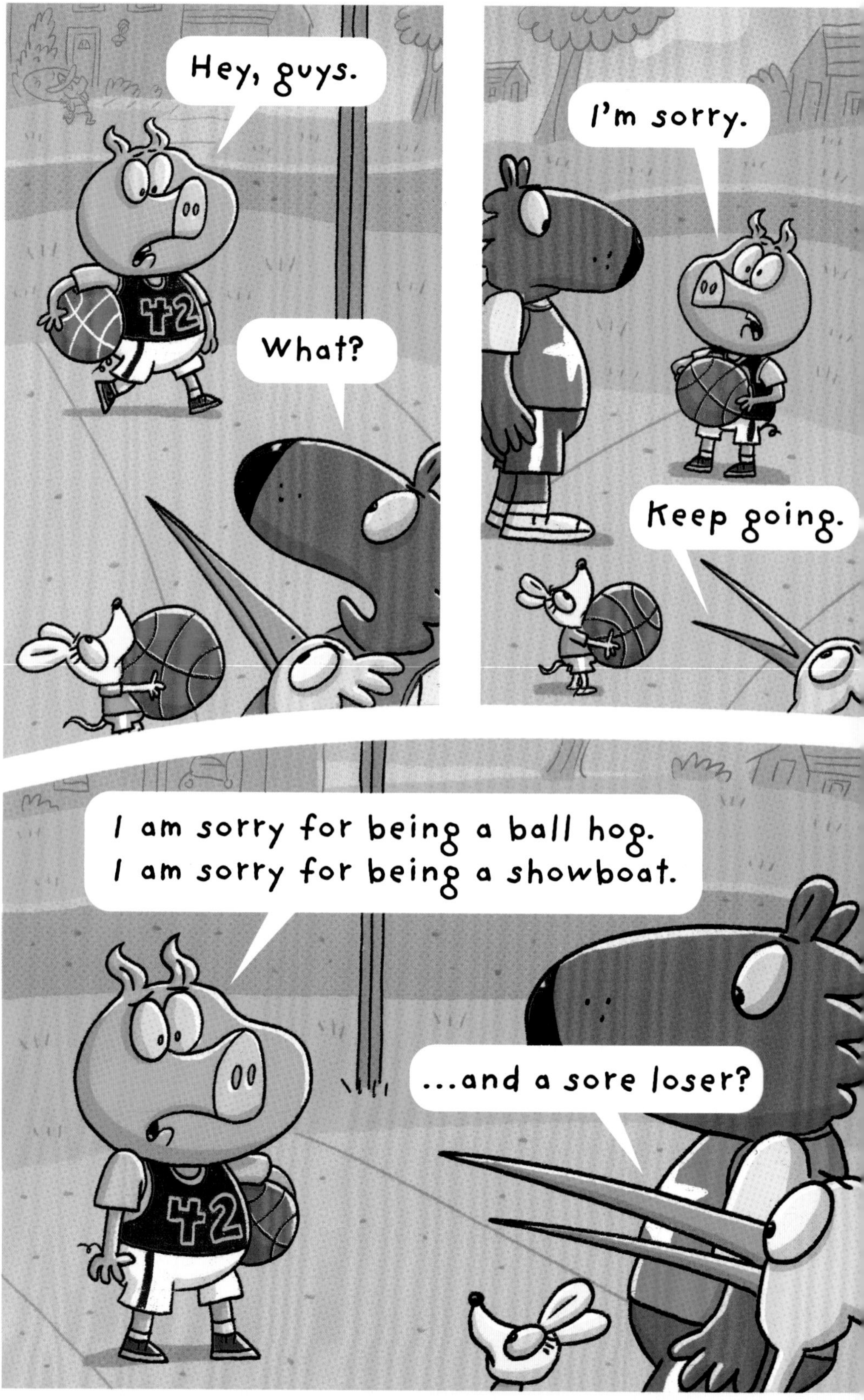

Hey, guys.
What?
I'm sorry.
Keep going.
I am sorry for being a ball hog.
I am sorry for being a showboat.
...and a sore loser?

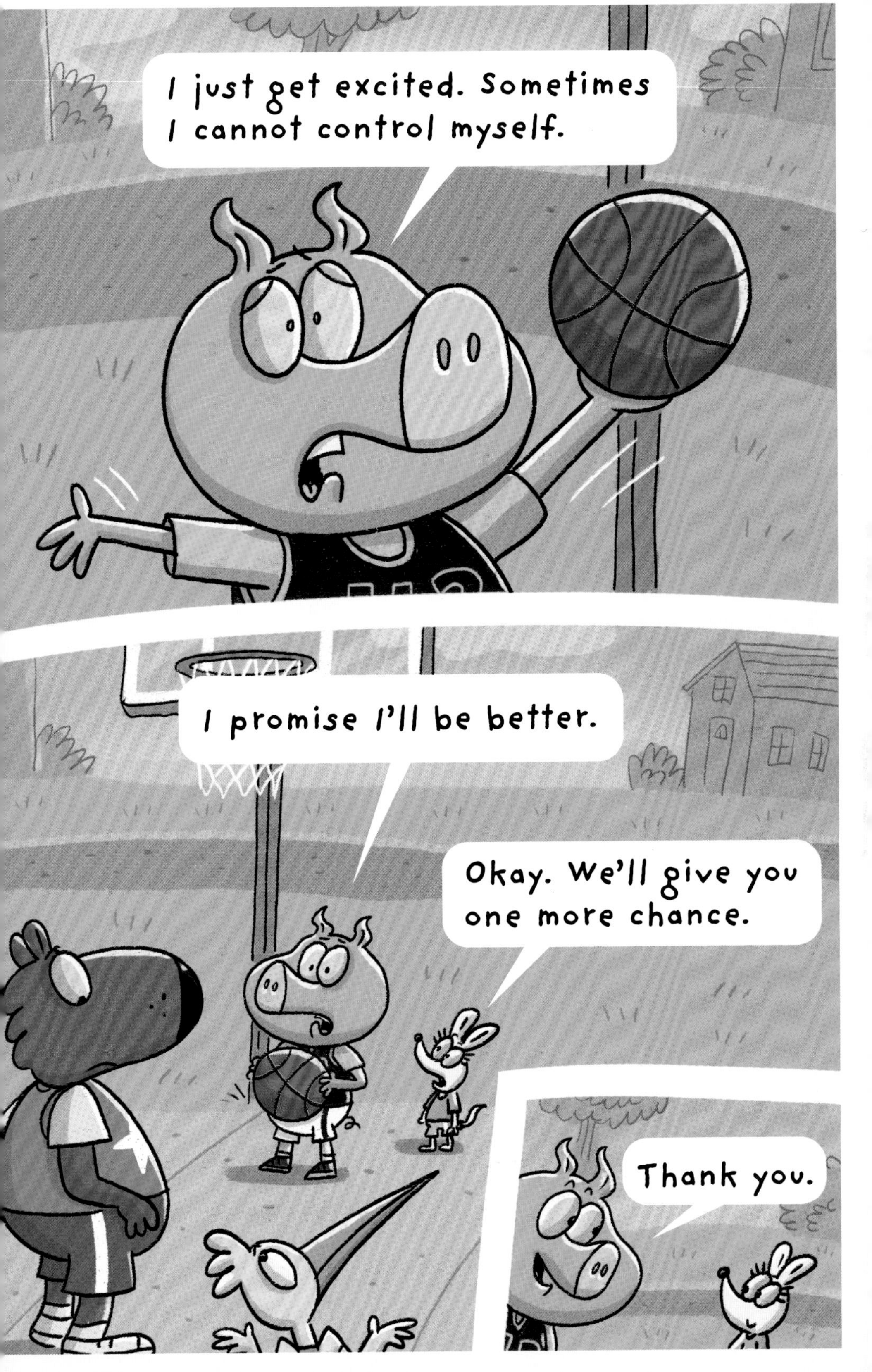
I just get excited. Sometimes I cannot control myself.
I promise I'll be better.
Okay. We'll give you one more chance.
Thank you.

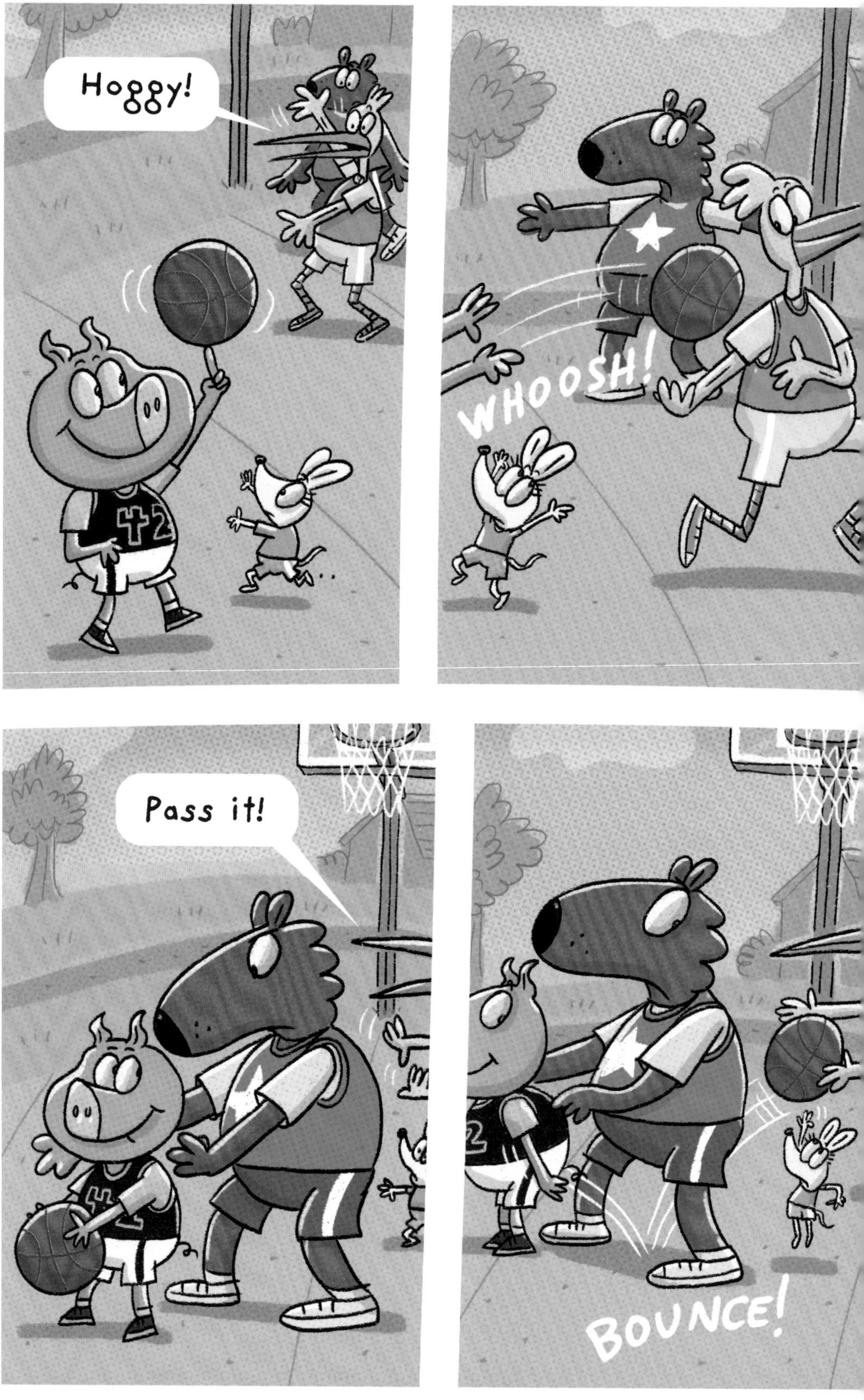
Hoggy!
WHOOSH!
Pass it!
BOUNCE!

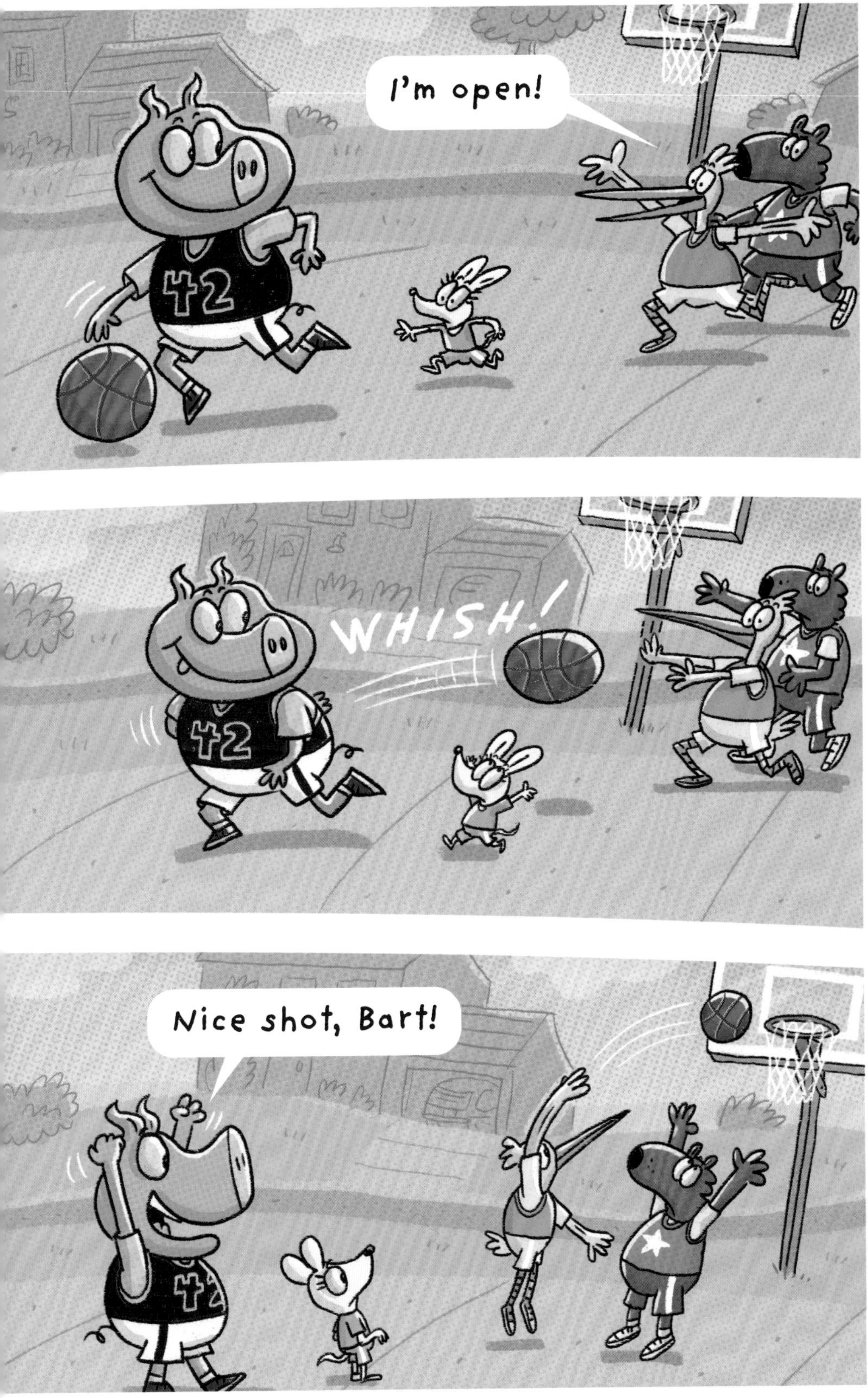
I'm open!
WHISH!
Nice shot, Bart!

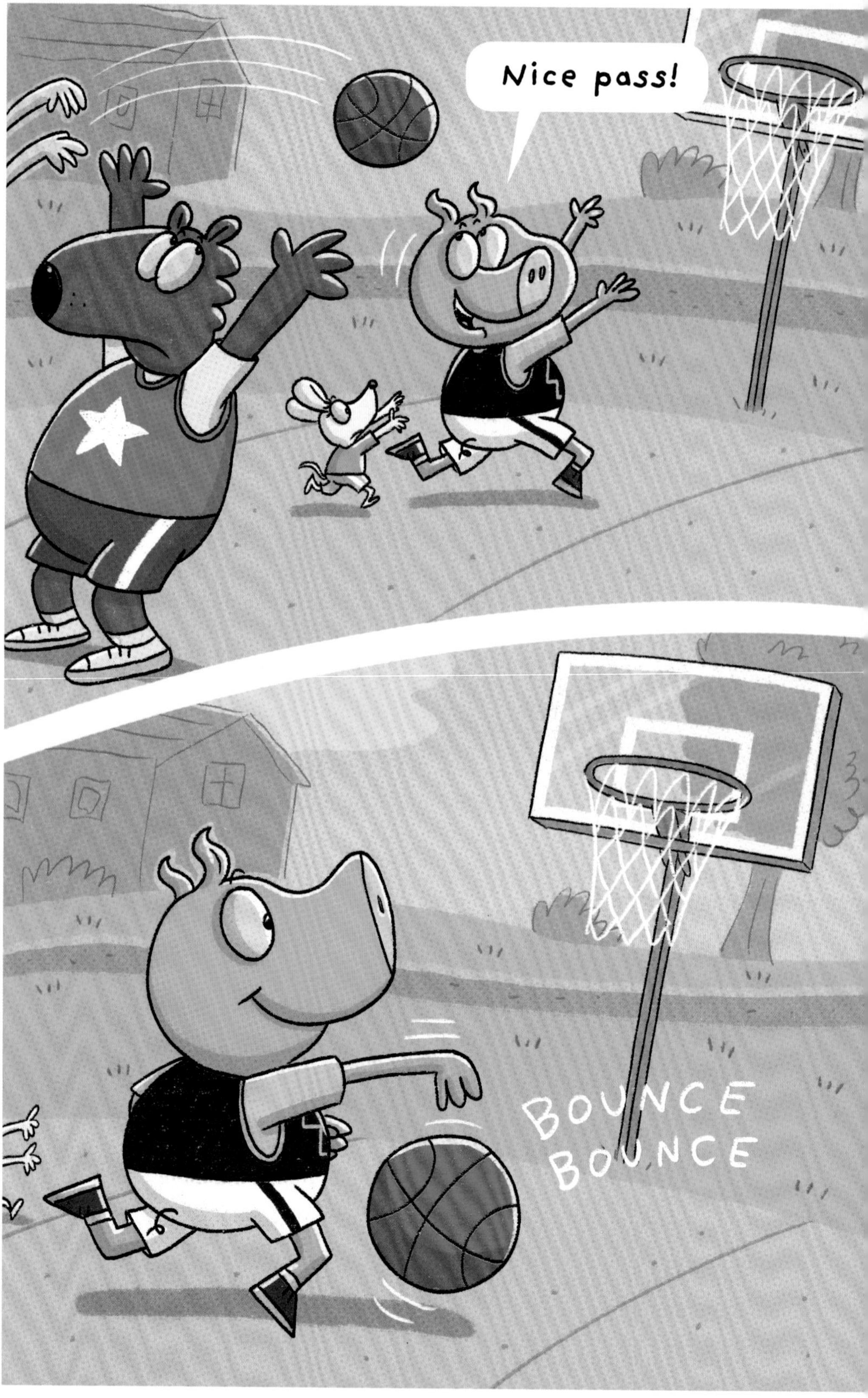

Nice pass!
BOUNCE
BOUNCE

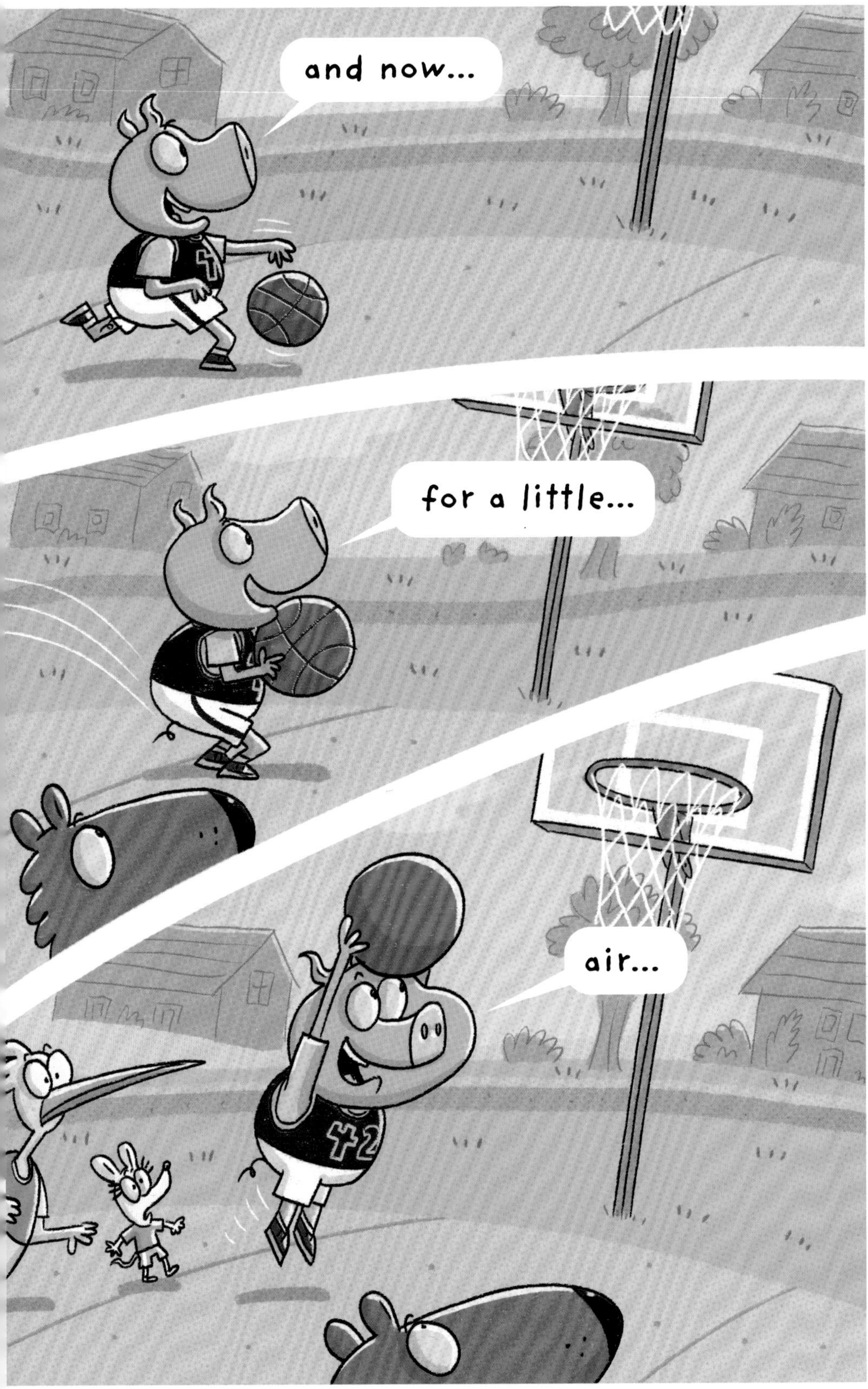
and now...
for a little...
air...

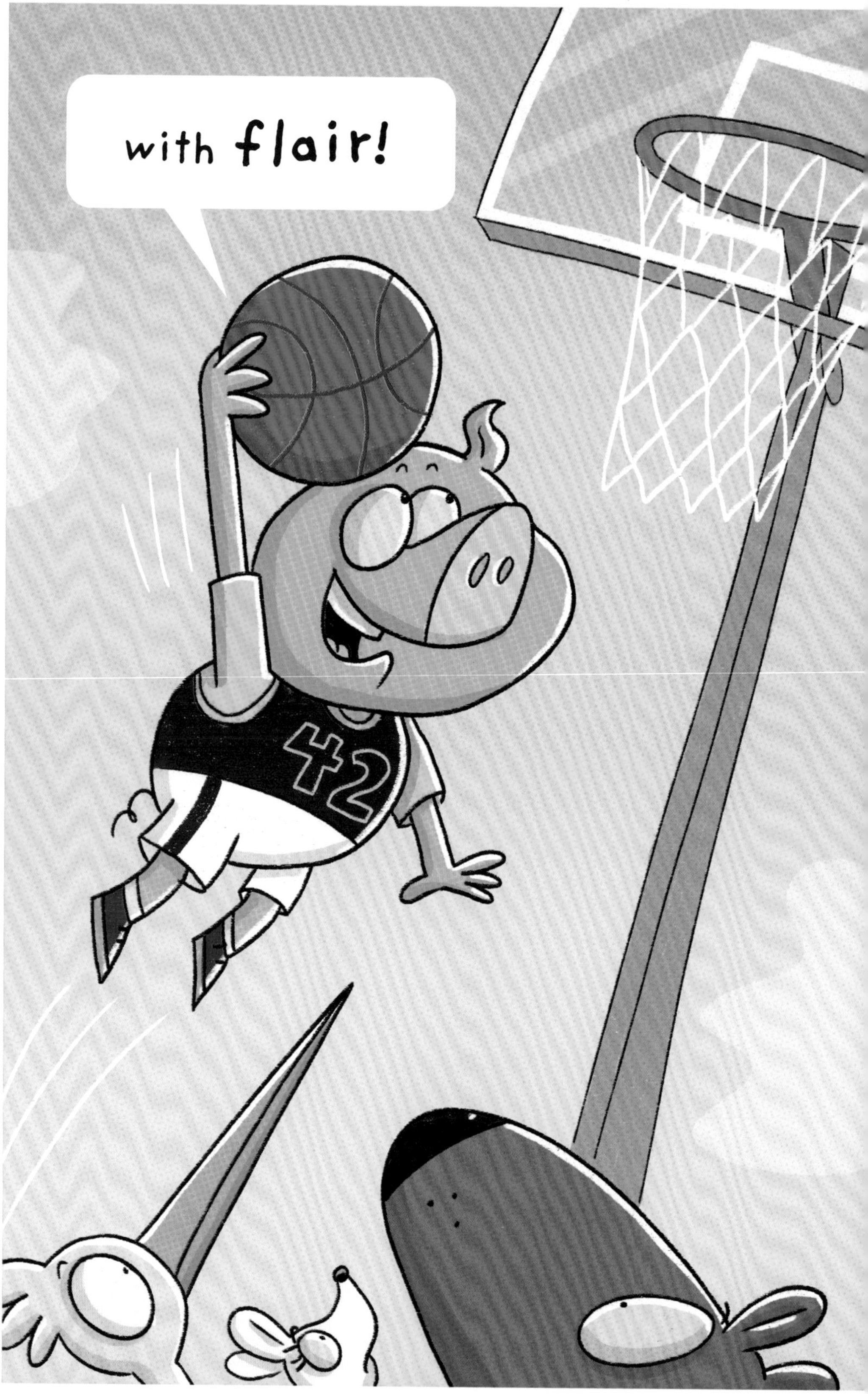
with flair!
42

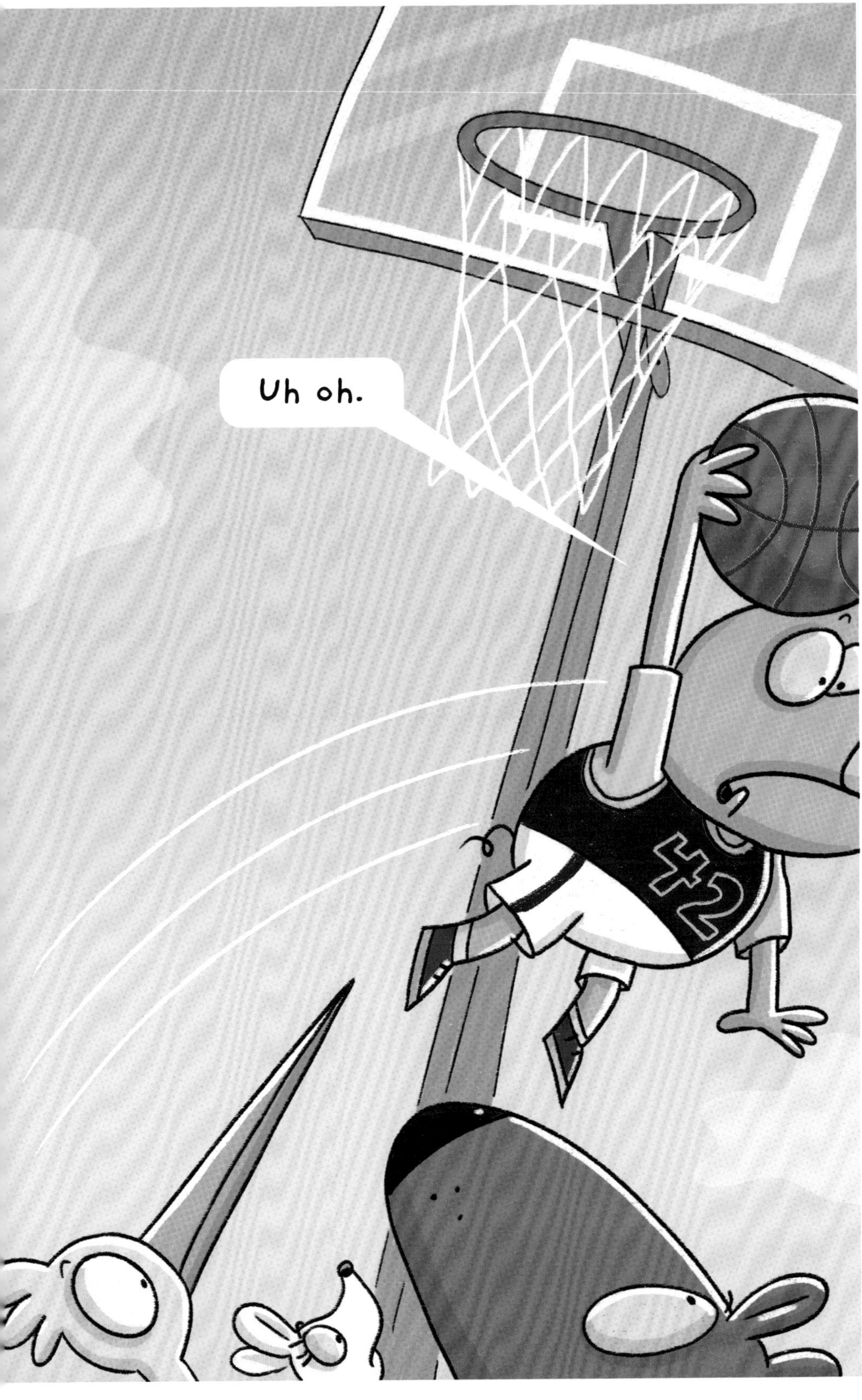
Uh oh.

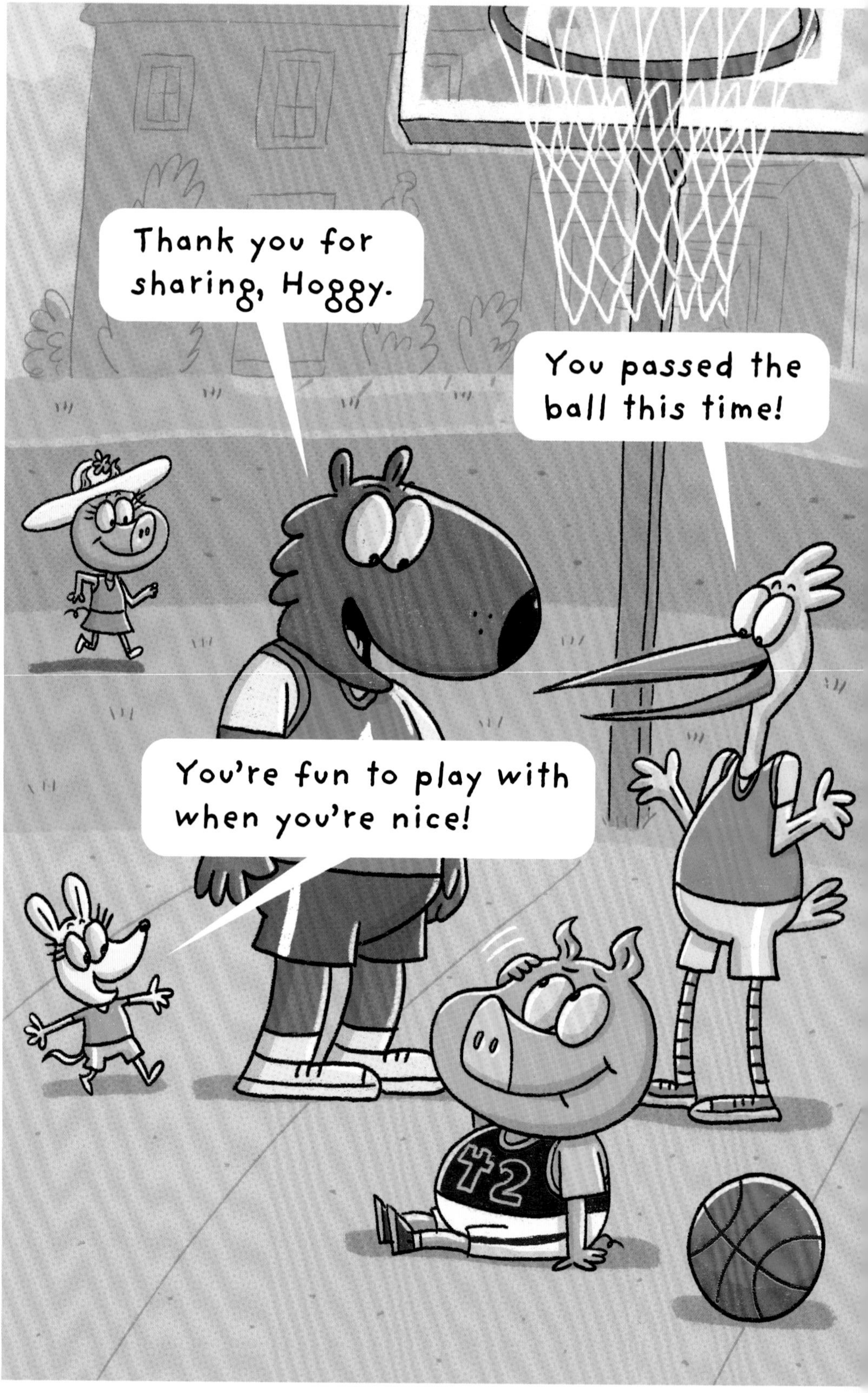

Thank you for sharing, Hoggy.
You passed the ball this time!
You're fun to play with when you're nice!

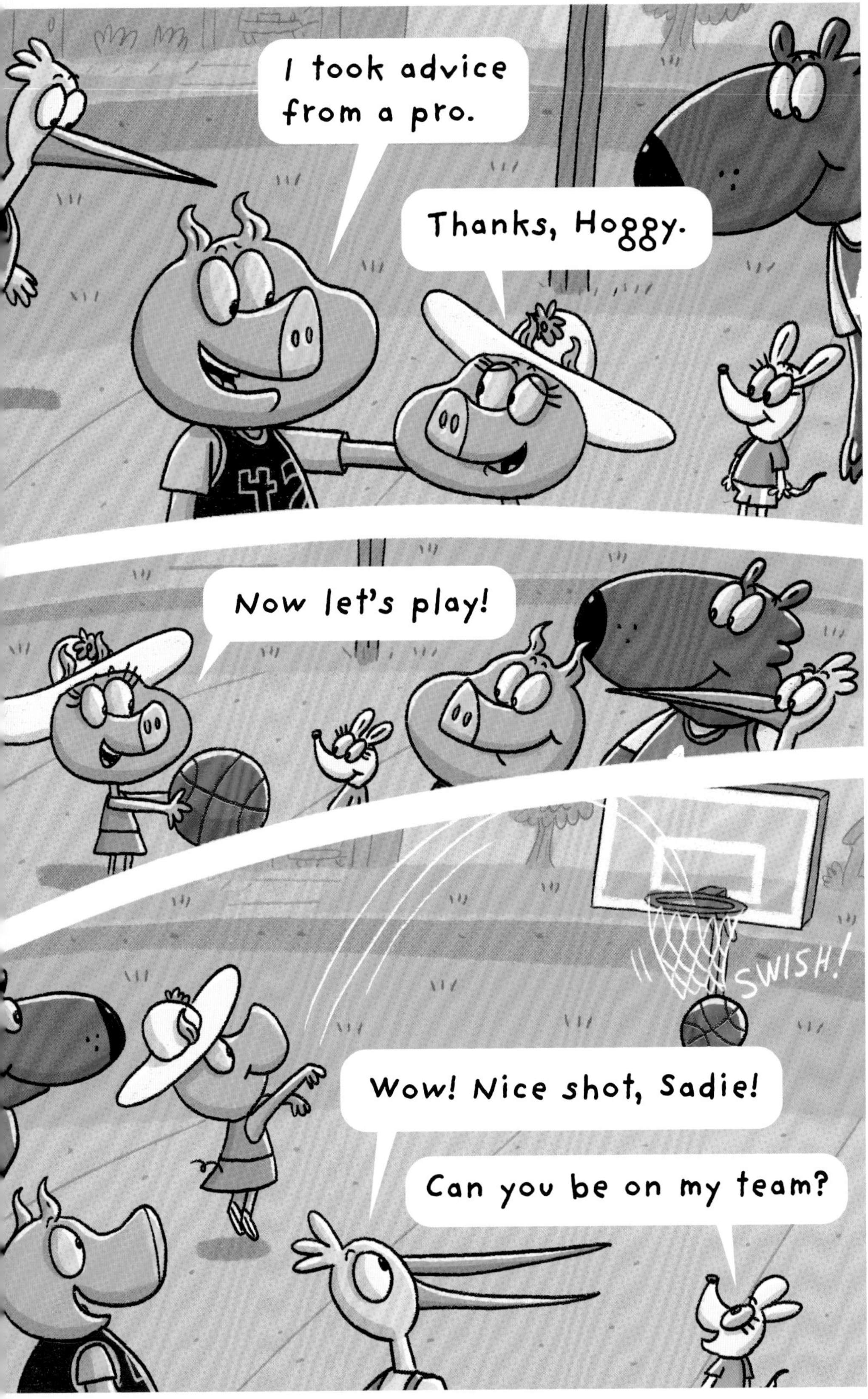
I took advice from a pro.
Thanks, Hoggy.
Now let's play!
SWISH!
Wow! Nice shot, Sadie!
Can you be on my team?

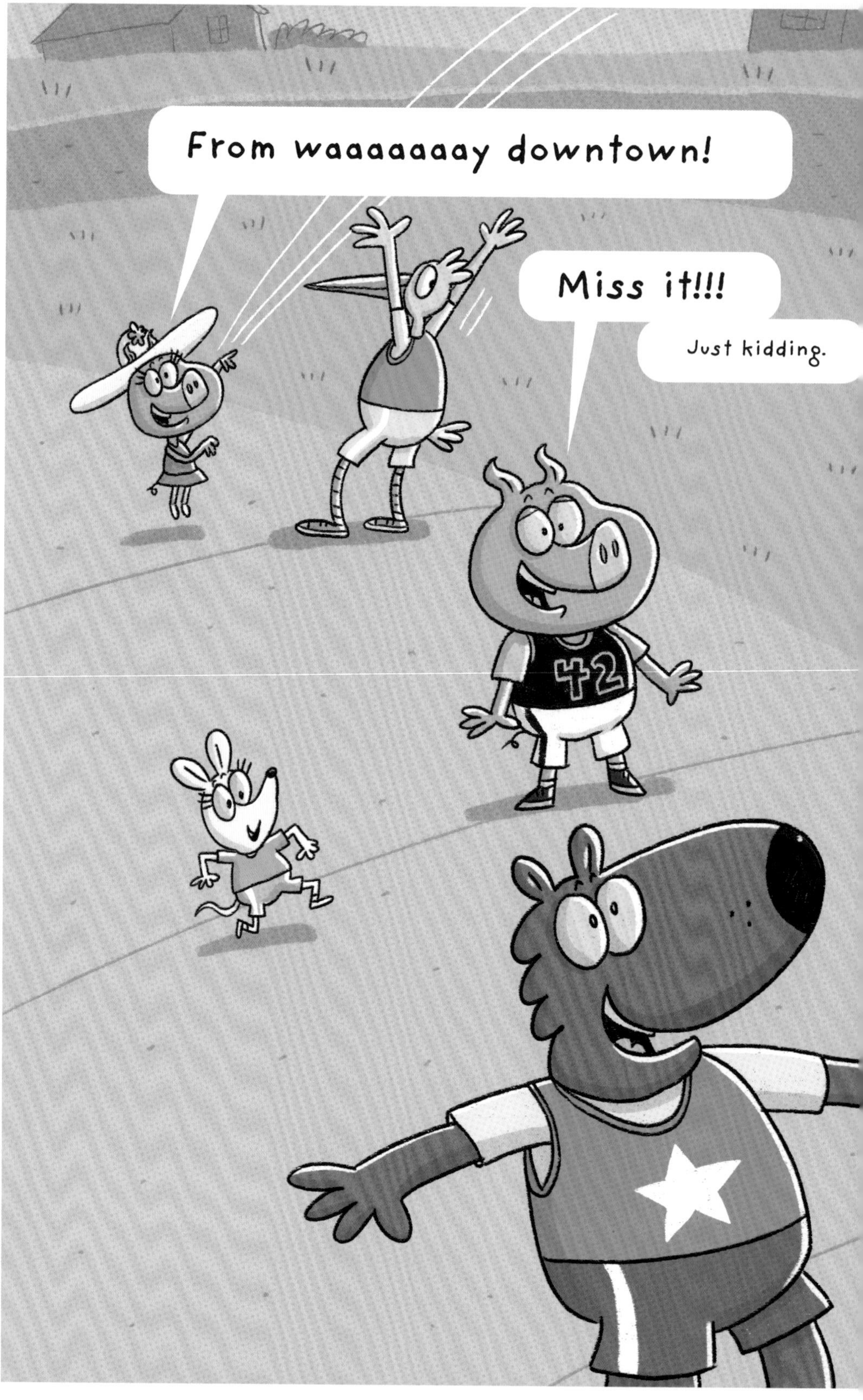
From waaaaaaay downtown!
Miss it!!!
Just kidding.
42

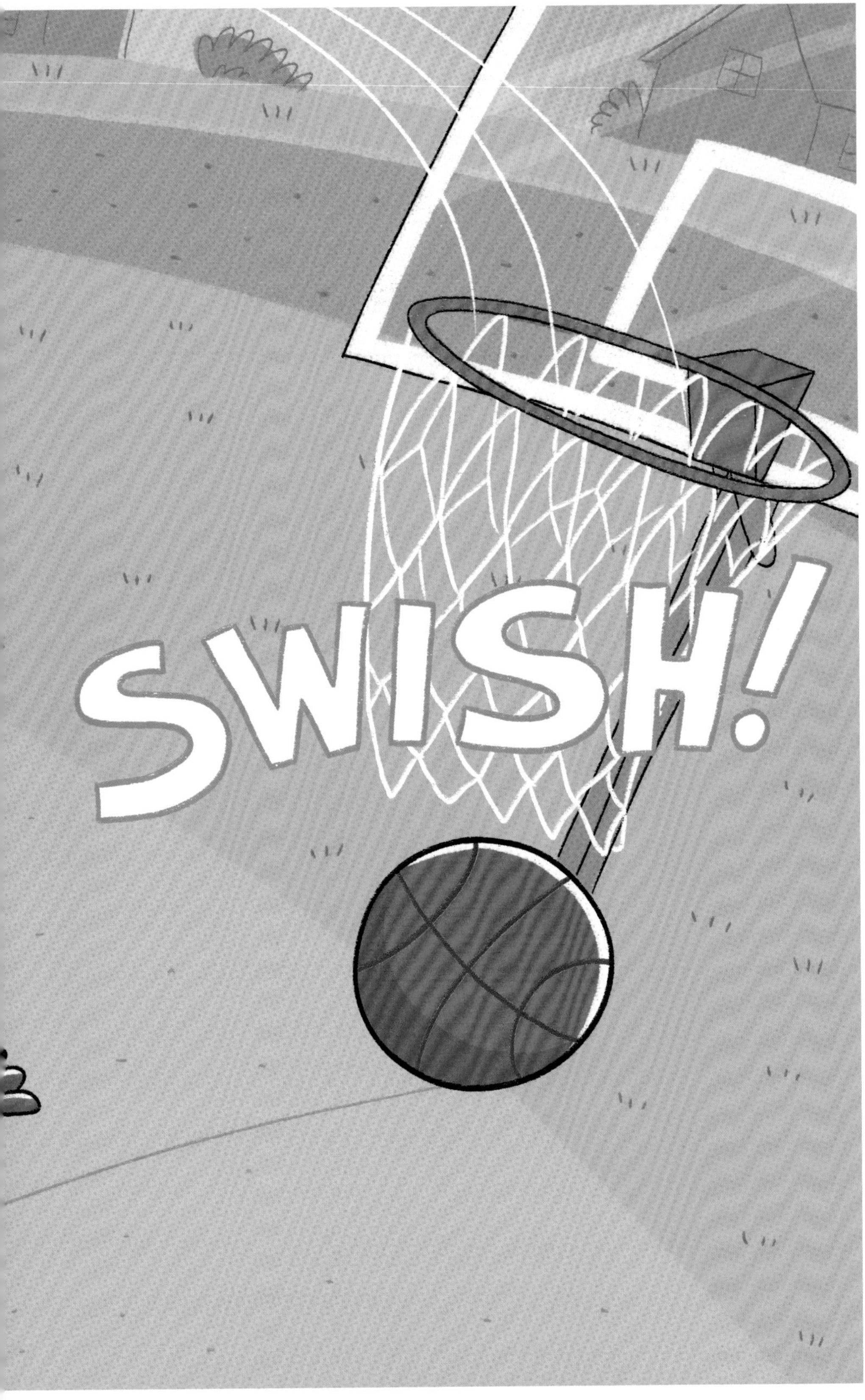
SWISH!

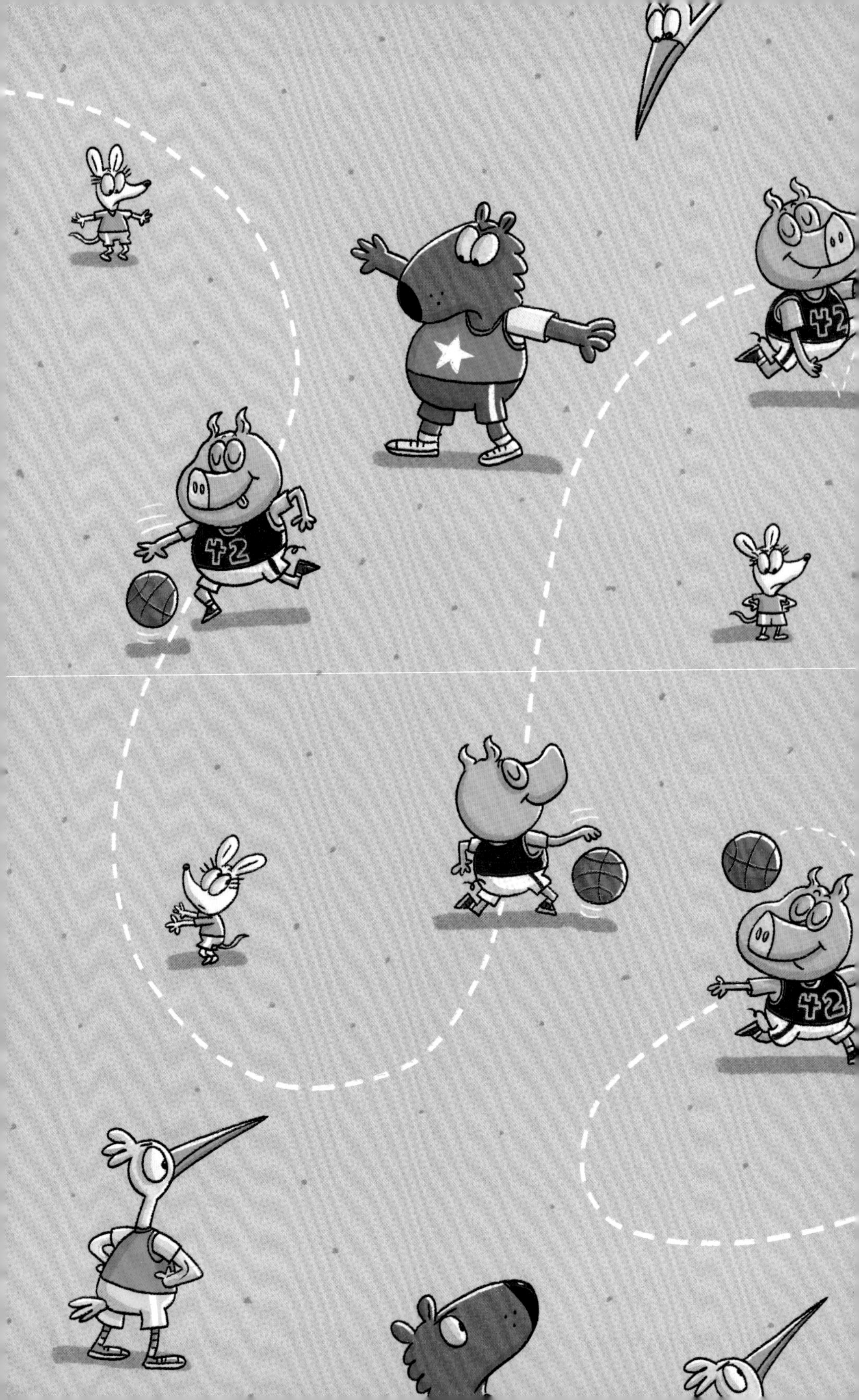
42
42
42